Perceval

Perceval
The Story of the Grail

Chrétien de Troyes

*Translated from the Old French
by Burton Raffel*

Afterword by Joseph J. Duggan

Yale University Press
New Haven & London

Set in Simoncini Garamond type by Tseng Information Systems, Durham, North Carolina. Printed in the United States of America.

Library of Congress Cataloging-in-Publication Data
Chrétien, de Troyes, 12th cent.
[Perceval le Gallois. English]
Perceval : the story of the grail / Chrétien de Troyes ; translated from the Old French by Burton Raffel ; afterword by Joseph J. Duggan.
    p.   cm.
Includes bibliographical references.
ISBN 978-0-300-07586-1 (pbk. : alk. paper)
1. Perceval (Legendary character)—Romances.   2. Romances—Translations into English.   3. Arthurian romances.   4. Grail—Romances.   I. Raffel, Burton.   II. Title.
PQ1447.E5R35   1999
841'.1—dc21   98-18938
                                                                     CIP

A catalogue record for this book is available from the British Library.

The paper in this book meets the guidelines for permanence and durability of the Committee on Production Guidelines for Book Longevity of the Council on Library Resources.

For Joe Duggan —
devoted scholar,
sensitive reader,
friend

Contents

Translator's Note

This is the fifth and last of Chrétien's great narratives I have translated. All have been published by Yale University Press, the first, *Yvain,* in 1987; the second, *Erec and Enide,* in 1996; the third and fourth, *Cligès* and *Lancelot,* in 1997. This version of *Perceval* concludes the enterprise.

Most of what needs to be explained about the technical aspects of the translation has long since been set out, in my Translator's Preface to *Yvain.* And as I also said there, "I will be content if this translation allows the modern English reader some reasonably clear view of Chrétien's swift, clear style, his wonderfully inventive story-telling, his perceptive characterizations and sure-handed dialogue, his racy wit and sly irony, and the vividness with which he evokes, for us his twentieth-century audiences, the emotions and values of a flourishing, vibrant world." I need only add that the longer I work with Chrétien, the more "modern" he seems to me, in many of his essential characteristics—which may help to explain why, as I said in concluding that prior Translator's Preface, "Chrétien is a delight to read—and to translate." Not easy, but definitely a delight.

Because, however, Chrétien apparently did not live to complete *Perceval,* and probably did not have the opportunity to make whatever final revisions might otherwise have been made, the structure and at times even the intent of this, the longest (and stylistically the richest and most far-ranging) of any of his *romans,* remains bafflingly unclear. What seems uncertain to the reader, let me affirm, is uncertain not only to the translator but also to the editor of the text, the late Daniel Poirion. The frequent bepuzzlement and befuddlement of M. Poirion's commentary is eloquent testimony to how little, as yet, we understand what Chrétien was up to—or whether, in fact, he was fully up to the task he appears to have set himself, in this his last poem. The final eight hundred lines or so, in my judgment, show a consistent and significant decline in Chrétien's *poetic* skills, his ability fully to focus on what he was creating. Aged or ill, he was still immensely superior, as a poet, to the "learned cleric" who finished *Lancelot.* But he was not entirely himself, and I have tried to allow the translation (like the last portion of *Lancelot*) to reflect this diminution in verse quality.

I have had constantly before me, in all the translations subsequent to *Yvain,* the two most recent editions of the Old French original, the 1994 *Oeuvres complètes,* edited for Gallimard's deservedly famous Pléiade series by M. Poirion and five collaborating scholars, and the 1994 complete *Romans,* edited for the Le Livre de Poche series, once again, by a team of scholars. Although I remain convinced of the general superiority of the Poirion texts (that for *Perceval* having been edited, once again, by M. Poirion himself), and have as before largely relied thereon, in a few places I have thought it better to follow the text edited for Le Livre de Poche by Charles Méla. Indeed, I have found Méla's modern French translation to be notably more accurate than that of Poirion, which editorializes and interprets, in my judgment, far too freely.

Université des Acadiens
Lafayette, Louisiana

Qui petit seme petit quialt,
Et qui auques recoillir vialt,
An tel leu sa semance espande
Que fruit a cent dobles li rande,
Car an terre qui rien ne vaut
Bone semance i seche et faut.

If you sow lightly, you reap
Lightly. And a good crop
Requires the kind of soil
Where seeds sprout a hundred-
Fold, for even good seed   5
Dies in dried-up ground.
What Chrétien sows—the seeds
He scatters—are the start of a story,
And he plants his words in such
Fine soil that he's bound to do well,   10
Because he's telling his tale
For the noblest man in the Holy
Roman Empire, Philip
Of Flanders—since despite the good things

They say of Alexander,   15
Count Philip is better, and I
Can prove it, for Alexander
Acquired all the evils
And vices of which the count
Was either free or innocent.   20
The count permits no vulgar
Joking, no wicked words,
And is pained by malicious prattle
Of anyone, no matter who.
He's fond of even-tempered   25
Justice, and good faith, and the Church,
And despises everything immoral.
His giving reaches in every
Direction, but no one knows
How far, for he gives without guile   30
Or greed, as Matthew said,
The left hand unaware
What the right hand does, hidden
Except from those who receive it
And from God, who sees our secrets   35
And can read our hearts and our bellies.
Why else does the Gospel say:
"Hide your good deeds from your left hand"?
The left hand, according to this
Tradition, is pompous pride,   40
Hypocritical and false.
And what does the right hand mean?
Charity, which never
Boasts, but conceals its goodness,
Lets no one know except Him   45
We call both God and Charity.

For God is Charity, and all
Who give with good hearts (Saint Paul
Has written, and I've read his words)
Live in God and God is   50
In them. The truth is plain:
Count Philip's good deeds amount
To the purest of pure charity,
For no one knows what he's given,
Or to whom, except his noble   55
Heart, which prompts his giving.
Would it be better to act
Like Alexander, indifferent
To charity, closed to goodness?
But no one believes such nonsense!   60
Chrétien's labors, the pains
He's taken, at the count's express
Command, to properly tell
This story (the best ever told
At the king's great court), will be worth   65
His struggles. It's the story of the Grail,*
From a book the count gave me:
And here's how Chrétien told it.
　　　The season was spring, trees
Were sprouting leaves, meadows   70
Were green, every morning
Birds sang in their own
Sweet language, and the world was joyful.
And the son of the widowed lady
Living alone in the Barren   75
Forest rose, and quickly

* A dish or plate, of the sort in which one might serve, say, a fish; see
lines 6421-22

Saddled his hunting horse
For himself, took three wooden
Spears and, thus equipped,
Rode away from his mother's   80
House, intending to check
On the plowmen sowing oats
In his mother's fields, a dozen
Oxen pulling six
Great plows. He entered the forest,   85
And the heart deep inside him
Leapt with joy at the sweet
Season and the happy sound
Of birds singing from trees
All around. Everything pleased him.   90
To savor this peaceful moment
He slipped the bridle from his horse's
Head, letting him graze
In the fresh green grass, then played
With the wooden spears he could throw   95
So well, hurling some
Behind him, some in front,
Some high in the air,
Then down, and up, and down
Again—until he heard   100
Five knights, all fully armed,
Riding through the forest
And making an immense racket
As, over and over, branches
Of oak trees and elms clattered   105
Against the heavy metal.
Mail shirts clinked and clanked,
Spears banged on shields,

And in shields and armor wood
Creaked and iron rang. 110
The boy could hear but could
Not see who was coming so quickly.
Stunned, he said to himself,
"By my soul, my mother was right,
Saying that in all the world 115
There was nothing so fearsome as devils!
And to teach me how to behave
She told me to cross myself
When I see them. But that's too much
To ask: instead of crossing 120
Myself I'll stick the biggest
And strongest with one of these wooden
Spears, and none of the others
Will come anywhere near me!"
      That's what he said to himself 125
Before he could see them. But once
They came into view, emerging
From the forest that hid them, and he saw
Their gleaming mail shirts and bright,
Shining helmets, and such shields 130
And spears as he'd never seen
In all his life, with their gleaming
Colors, green and purple,
Gold and blue and silver,
Lit by the sun, they seemed to him 135
Wonderfully handsome and good.
And he said, "O God, forgive me!
I see angels here
In front of me! I sinned against You—
What wickedness I spoke!— 140

When I called them devils. Those weren't
Fairy tales my mother
Told me, saying that except
For God Himself angels
Were the loveliest creatures in existence.   145
But that one, I think, who seems
So lovely that none of the others
Boasts a tenth of his beauty,
That one must be God.
And hasn't my mother told me   150
That God must be loved and adored,
Honored and implored, bowed down to?
I will adore that one,
And all the angels with him."
        So he threw himself down   155
On the ground, and knelt, chanting
Every prayer he knew
(Taught him by his mother). And seeing
How he prayed, the leader of the knights
Called out: "Stop! Wait!   160
This boy, seeing us coming,
Has fallen to the ground in fright.
Should we come riding at him,
All together, I think
He's likely to die of fear —   165
And a corpse won't be able
To answer a thing I ask."
So the others stopped, and their leader
Hurried forward, greeting
The boy with reassuring   170
Words: "Don't be afraid,
Fellow!" "By the God I believe in,"

Said the boy, "I'm not. Are you
God?" "Hardly, by my faith."
"Then what *are* you?" "A knight."   175
"I've never met a knight,"
Said the boy, "and I've never seen one,
Or spoken with one, or heard one—
But you're more beautiful than God.
I wish I could be like you—   180
Shining, just like you!"
At this, the knight came closer
To the boy, and asked, "Have you seen
Five knights and three young girls
Today, anywhere near here?"   185
But the boy had other things
On his mind, and other questions
To ask. Grasping the knight's
Spear, he said, "Your beautiful
Lordship, known as a knight: 190
What's this you're carrying here?"
"I'm not learning much
From this fellow," said the knight. "That's clear.
My dear young friend, I'm seeking
Information from you—   195
And you're asking the questions!
All right, I'll tell you. It's my spear."
"You mean," said the boy, "you spear things
With this, as I do with my sticks?"
"Good lord, what a fool you are!   200
It isn't for throwing, but striking."
"Then any one of my sticks—
See them, right there?—is better
Than this. When I want to kill

A bird, or maybe an animal,   205
I do it from as far away
As a crossbow arrow can carry."
"I really don't care," said the knight.
"Now answer the question I asked you:
Do you know where those knights have gone?   210
Have you seen the girls I'm seeking?"
Taking hold of the shield,
The boy asked, bluntly,
"What do you use this for?"
"What kind of game is this?   215
You set me all sorts of questions
And never answer mine!
In the name of God, I expected
Answers from you, not questions:
You act as if I'm your teacher!   220
Well, no matter, I'll tell you
Anyway: I want you to be pleased.
This thing I'm carrying is a shield."
"It's called a shield?" "Exactly.
And it's not to be despised,   225
Believe me: it's been a faithful
Friend, stopping any
Arrow or spear that tries
To hurt me. It stops them all—
And that's why I carry this shield."   230
        Then those who'd been hanging back,
Waiting for their chief, came hurrying
Up the road, asking him
Anxiously, "My lord, what
On earth is this Welshman telling you?"   235
"As God is my witness, his wits

Are distinctly scattered. Whatever
I ask him, point blank, he answers
Sideways, and off the mark,
Asking the names of things   240
And how they're used." "My lord,
Believe me, the Welsh can't help it:
They're all born like that,
Crazy as cows in a pasture.
And this one's dumb as an ox.   245
It's silly to stop for him,
Letting him babble away
And wasting precious time."
"I'm not so sure," said their chief.
"May God look down on me, now!   250
Before we ride on our way
I'll tell him whatever he wants,
And I won't ride on till I do."
He turned to the boy once more:
"Fellow," he said, "please,   255
Just tell me: did you meet those five knights,
And the girls I asked you about?
Did you see them riding by?"
The boy took hold of his mail shirt
And gave it a tug. "Tell me,   260
Good sir," he said, "what's this
You're wearing?" "You really don't know?"
"Not at all." "This is my mail shirt:
It's just as heavy as iron."
"Is it made of iron?" "See   265
For yourself." "I really don't know.
But how lovely it is, God save me!
Why do you wear it? What

Does it do?" "That's easy enough:
If you tried to pierce me with one   270
Of your sticks, or an arrow, you couldn't
Do me a bit of harm."
"In that case, Sir Knight, may stags
And does never get
These mail shirts, or I'll never kill   275
Another; I'll give up hunting!"
The knight said, yet again,
"In the name of God, fellow,
Can't you give me news
Of those knights, and the girls who were with them?"   280
And the boy, who didn't know
Very much, answered, "Were you born
With this shirt?" "Good lord, no.
No one could be born like this!"
"Then how do you come to have it?"   285
"I could tell you the whole story."
"Please do." "Gladly. King Arthur
Made me a knight, just five
Days ago, and gave me
All my armor and weapons.   290
Now tell me what became
Of those knights who rode past here,
Leading three girls behind them.
Were they jogging along, or hurrying?"
Said the boy, "Sir, just look   295
At that wood, way up high,
Around that mountain. The Valdonne
Pass cuts through, up there."
"What are you telling me, friend?"
"My mother's plowmen are working   300

The land, up there. And if
These people came by, they'd surely
Have seen them. They'll tell you, if you ask."
The knights agreed to follow
Behind, if he'd lead the way   305
And guide them to his mother's plowmen.
        So the boy fetched his horse
And took them where the plowmen were turning
Over the soil and sowing
His mother's fields with oats.   310
And as soon as they saw their lady's
Son, they trembled with fear.
Do you know what made them afraid?
They saw the knights who were with him,
Riding with weapons and armor,   315
And they knew the questions he'd asked them,
And all the things he'd been told,
And now he'd want to be
A knight, and his mother would go mad,
For they knew how hard she'd worked   320
To keep him from ever seeing
A knight, or learning about them.
Then the boy asked the workmen,
"Have any of you seen five knights
And three girls go riding by?"   325
"They spent the day going down
These passes," the plowmen replied.
And the boy said to the knight
Who'd told him so many things:
"Sir, the knights and the girls   330
Came riding along this way.
But now, tell me about

The king who makes people knights,
And where I'm likely to find him."
"Fellow," said the knight, "I can tell you   335
The king's court is at Carlisle,
And just five days ago
That's where he was, because
I was there, and I saw him.
But if he's gone when you get there,   340
There'll be plenty of people to guide you.
No matter how far he's traveled,
They'll be glad to help you find him.
And now I ask you to tell me, please,
What name I should know you by?"   345
"Sir," was the answer, "I'll tell you.
I'm called Dear Son." "Dear Son?
Yes, but I'm sure you have
Another name." "Oh yes.
I'm called Dear Brother." "I believe you.   350
But if you'll tell me the truth
I'd like to know your real name."
"Sir," was the answer, "I'll tell you,
Of course. They call me Good Master."
"A really fine name, by God!   355
And you have no other?" "No,
I've never had any other."
"I'm hearing strange things, by God,
The strangest I've ever heard—
And I'll never hear any stranger!"   360
And then, anxious to catch
The others, who had gone ahead,
He galloped off like the wind.
And the boy went hurrying home

To the house he'd always lived in,   365
Where his mother was waiting, and worrying,
For her son had not returned
When he should. She felt immense joy
The moment she saw him, nor could she
Conceal her happiness: loving him   370
With a deep maternal passion,
She ran to greet him, crying
"Dear son, dear son," a hundred times
Over. "Dear son, how my heart
Hurt, when you didn't come home!   375
The pain was so sharp that only
A little more and I might have
Died. Where have you been?"
"Where, mother? I'll tell you
Everything, just as it happened,   380
For the things I saw today
Made me tremendously happy.
Mother, you've always told me
That the angels of our Lord in Heaven
Were so wonderfully lovely that nothing   385
In all of Nature, nothing
In the world, could be more beautiful."
"Dear son, I'll say it again,
Just as I've said it before,
For it's true." "Mother, don't say that—   390
For haven't I seen, in the Barren
Forest, just now, the most beautiful
Creatures—far more beautiful
Than God Himself or all
His angels." His mother embraced him,   395
And said, "Dear son, may God

Protect you, for you make me terribly
Afraid. What you've seen, I think,
Were angels that all men fear,
For they kill whoever they meet."   400
"Oh no, mother, no!
They say they're called 'knights.' "
The moment he pronounced this word
His mother fainted away.
And when she recovered her senses,   405
She spoke in sorrow and anger:
"Oh Lord, what misery I feel!
My dear sweet son, I've worked
So hard to keep you from all knowledge
Of knighthood, protect you from seeing   410
Such creatures or hearing the word.
You would have been a knight,
Dear son, had it pleased God
To keep your father and all
Your other friends alive.   415
No braver, more worthy knight
Ever existed, more famous
And more feared, anywhere in all
The Western Islands, than your father.
Dear son, you're entitled to boast   420
Of the highest, purest lineage
Both on his side and on mine,
For I, too, was born
Of knights, the best in this land.
Nowhere in the Islands is there   425
A family better than mine—
But now the best have fallen:
As everyone knows, noble

Men who uphold the highest
Standards of courage and honor   430
Are these days hard to find.
Wicked, shameful, and lazy
Men don't die—never!
It's the good who are killed.
Your father, let me tell you,   435
Was wounded between the legs*
And his whole body was crippled.
All the lands, and the immense
Treasure his bravery had won
Began to fall away,   440
And he died terribly poor.
The best and bravest knights
Were all impoverished and deserted
And exiled, after the death
Of Uther Pendragon, our king   445
And father of Arthur. Their lands
Were pillaged and ruined, and the poor
People who worked them were beaten
Down. All who were able
Fled. Your father owned   450
This house, here in the Barren
Forest. He could not flee.
He was hurriedly carried here
In a litter: there was no other refuge.
And you, who were still so tiny,   455
Had two beautiful brothers.
You were barely two years old,
Still a babe at the breast.
        "When your brothers were grown, at your father's

* That is, "castrated"; some manuscripts offer alternative readings

Advice and with his help   460
They were sent to two royal courts
To earn armor and horses
And weapons. The oldest served
The king of Escavalon
Until he was made a knight.   465
And his younger brother went
To King Ban of Gomeret:
They were both made knights on the same
Day, and on that day
Both of them started back   470
To their father's home, here,
To celebrate with him
And with me, but they never came,
For both of them fell in combat.
Battle killed them both,   475
And left me in sorrow and pain.
A strange thing happened
To the oldest: ravens and crows
Pecked out his eyes. They found
His body lying like that.   480
Sorrow for his sons killed
Their father, and since their deaths
Life has been bitter for me.
You are all the comfort
I have, and all that's worthwhile;   485
There's no one else in my life.
God has left me nothing
Else that can give me pleasure."
        But the boy barely heard
A word his mother said.
"Have them bring me food!"   490

He ordered. "What are you saying?
All I know is I'm going
As fast as I can to the king
Who makes knights, no matter what!"   495
His mother did all she could
To hold him back, getting
Everything ready—a shirt
Of coarse hemp and breeches
Cut according to Welsh   500
Fashion (in which, I believe,
Breeches and stockings are sewn
Together), and a deer-hide tunic
And a cape with a tight-fitting hood.
   And thus his mother equipped him.   505
It took her roughly three days—
But she couldn't hold him a day
Longer. She spilled out tears
And kisses, weeping as she hugged him,
Saying, "How sad it makes me,   510
Dear son, to see you leaving!
You'll go to the king's court
And you'll ask him for armor and weapons.
No one will tell him not to:
He'll give you what you need, I know   515
He will. But when it comes
To using what you've gotten, what then?
How will you know what to do,
When you've never done it before,
And never seen it done?   520
You'll manage badly, I know it:
As poorly prepared as you are,
How can you *not* do badly?

How can one know what has never
Been learned? How can one *not* know   525
What has often been seen and heard?
          "Let me teach you something,
Dear son, you'd do well to remember—
And if you do, believe me,
It will bring you endless rewards.   530
My son, God willing, you'll soon
Be a knight. Congratulations.
Should you find a lady in need—
Anywhere, near or far—
Or a girl in need of protection,   535
Always offer your aid,
If they ask it, for there's no honor
That isn't built on that base.
A knight indifferent to a lady's
Honor has lost his own.   540
But serve ladies and girls
And honor will always be yours.
And if you court a woman,
Be careful you don't harass her:
Do nothing that might displease her.   545
A kiss means a lot to a girl,
So if she allows you a kiss
Don't ask for anything more:
Renounce it, I beg you, in my name.
But if there's a ring on her finger   550
Or an alms purse buckled to her belt,
And for the sake of love she gives you
Either, I think it good
To wear whatever she gives you.
It's proper to accept a ring—   555

Yes, and an alms purse, too.
But I've more to tell you, dear son.
When you're in lodgings or on
The road, don't wait too long
To ask your companions' names: 560
Learn their names, complete
And entire, for a name tells you
A man. Converse with the brave,
Dear son; ride with the brave;
For the brave never deceive   565
Those with whom they keep company.
And above all else, I beg you,
Go to monasteries
And churches and pray to our Lord
That you live this worldly life   570
Well, and are honored, until
You reach the right end to your days."
"Mother," he asked. "What's a church?"
"A place where one worships the Creator
Of heaven and earth, the Maker   575
Of all living things."
"And a monastery?" "The same:
A beautiful, sacred building
That houses treasures and dead saints,
And where we consecrate   580
The sacrifice of Jesus,
Who suffered at the hands of the Jews—
Betrayed and falsely judged,
He suffered the anguish of death
For all men and women,   585
Whose souls would have gone to Hell
Once they left these earthly bodies,

But He saved them from the Devil.
They nailed His body to the cross,
First beaten, then crucified;   590
He wore a crown of thorns.
You'll go to a monastery
To hear the prayers and masses
With which we honor our Lord."
"From the moment I leave you, I'll be very   595
Happy to go to churches
And monasteries," said her son.
"Mother, I promise you that."
          He could not wait any longer,
But said farewell. And his mother   600
Wept, as he sat in his saddle.
His clothes were those the Welsh
Peasants usually wear
(Including their clumsy leather
Shoes); wherever he went   605
He carried three sharp wooden sticks,
And would have taken them with him,
Now, but his mother took away
Two, saying he looked
Too Welsh. She'd infinitely rather   610
Have taken all three, if she could.
His right hand held a willow
Switch, for hurrying his horse.
Weeping bitterly, his mother
Kissed him (for she loved him dearly),   615
And prayed that God would guide him.
"Dear son," she said, "may the Lord
Grant you more joy, wherever
You go, than you leave behind you."

He hadn't gone as far   620
As a pebble could be thrown, when he looked
Back and saw that his mother,
On the other side of the bridge,
Had fallen to the ground, unconscious,
And lay as if stone dead,   625
But he bent and whipped his horse,
Hard, with his willow stick,
And the animal stretched his legs
And carried him, at a rapid gallop,
Into the dark forest.   630
And then he rode straight on,
From dawn till the day was over.
He slept on the forest floor,
That night, and woke with the light.
      He rose as the birds began   635
To sing, and mounted his horse,
Then rode without stopping until
He saw a tent pitched
In a beautiful meadow, near
Where a brook bubbled from the ground.   640
The tent was gorgeously made,
Half bright red, half
Embroidered with golden stripes,
And a gold eagle at the top.
The eagle glittered, clear   645
And bright and red, in the sun's
Hot rays, reflections from which
Went splashing across the meadow
And the rest of the tent (more beautiful
Than any in the world), which was carefully   650
Encircled, in the Welsh style,

With structures built of branches
And leaves. He hurried toward that tent,
Exclaiming, even before
He reached it, "God, I see   655
Your dwelling! How wrong I would be
Not to stop and adore You!
And how right my mother was,
Telling me monasteries
And churches were the loveliest things   660
In this world, instructing me always
To go out of my way, when I found one,
To worship my God and creator.
I'll stop here and offer Him prayers,
And perhaps, since that's what I need,   665
He'll give me something to eat."
　　　　He reached the tent, which was open.
And right in the middle he saw
A bed, covered with a silken
Cloth, and on it, all   670
Alone, a girl was sleeping,
With no one to keep her company,
For the girls who served her had gone
To pick fresh new flowers
To scatter around the tent.   675
That was their usual custom.
As the boy entered the tent
His horse stumbled so badly
That the girl heard and, waking
Suddenly, was astonished to see him.   680
And the boy, innocent fool
That he was, said, "Girl, I greet you,
As my mother taught me I should.

That's what she taught me: always
Greet a girl, no matter   685
Where you happen to find her."
        The girl shook with fear,
Convinced he was out of his head,
And sure she'd proven herself
A fool, to be found all alone.   690
"Fellow," she said, "Be gone,
Leave, before my friend
Finds you." "But first I'll kiss you,"
Said the boy, "no matter what,
Just as my mother taught me."   695
"Oh no, you won't, by God!"
Said the girl, "Not if I
Can help it! Leave, before
He finds you, or you're good as dead."
Awkwardly (not knowing   700
Any better), the boy
Clasped her in his strong arms,
And lay full length above her,
While she struggled as hard as she could,
Trying to get away.   705
But her best defense was useless,
Because—as the story tells us—
He kissed her twenty times,
Or even more, until
He suddenly saw the ring   710
On her finger, the emerald glowing.
"And my mother told me," he said,
"You'd be wearing a precious ring,
And that's all you'd give me, nothing
Else. I'd like that ring."   715

"You'll never have my ring,"
Said the girl. "Never, never,
Unless you take it by force."
The boy grasped her hand
And forced it open, then took   720
The ring off her finger
And put it on his own.
"Ah, that's fine!" he said.
"Now I can leave, well paid.
And your kisses, you know,   725
Are better than any I ever
Had from my mother's chamber
Maids: your mouth tastes better."
          The girl was weeping as she answered:
"Don't carry off my ring!   730
You'll leave me in terrible trouble
And, sooner or later, I swear it,
You'll pay with your life. Please listen."
Nothing she said, not a single
Word, touched his heart,   735
But since he still hadn't eaten
He felt himself dying of hunger.
He found a flask, full
Of wine, and a silver cup,
And saw, on a woven mat,   740
A shining new white napkin,
And found, when he raised it, three fresh-baked
Venison pies—a meal
That, because of the pangs of hunger
Gnawing inside him, he couldn't   745
Find unpleasing. Breaking
One of the pies, he gulped it

Down, then drank clear
Good wine from the silver cup,
Again, and again, and deeply,   750
Then said, "Girl, I won't
Be gobbling all these pies:
Come eat, they're very good.
There's one apiece for us,
And a whole one left on the plate."   755
But the girl never stopped crying,
In spite of his invitation;
Not only didn't she answer,
But she cried even harder,
Twisting her hands in fury.   760
But the boy went on eating
And drinking, till he'd had enough.
Then he covered the pies that were left,
And quickly took his leave,
Commending her, like it   765
Or not, to the care of God
"God be with you, good friend!"
He said. "And don't be angry
Because I've taken your ring:
Before it's my time to die   770
I plan to pay you back.
And now I bid you farewell."
But the girl went on weeping
And said she couldn't commend *him*
To God, for on his account   775
She'd suffer more shame and sorrow
Than any slave ever knew.
As long as she lived, she'd never
Accept help from him:

"Believe me, you've betrayed me!"   780
      And so she stayed there, weeping.
But she hadn't long to wait:
Her lover came home from the forest.
He saw the horse's hoofprints,
Leading to the house, and was worried,   785
Especially finding the girl
In tears: "Young lady, judging
By these signs I see, you've had
A knight in the house, while I
Was away." "Oh no, I swear it,   790
Only a Welsh boy,
A vulgar pest, and a fool,
Who drank as much of your wine
As he wanted, and more, and tasted
Your three venison pies."   795
"And that, pretty lady, is why
You're crying? He could have eaten
And drunk everything and not bothered
Me." "But there's more, my lord.
My ring is the problem, as well: 800
He took it, and carried it off.
I'd rather have died, indeed
I would, than let him take it!"
Now this disturbed the knight;
And jealousy bit at his heart.   805
"By God," he said, "this
Is too much! But since he's got it,
Let him keep it. But I think there's more.
Whatever it is, don't hide it."
"My lord," she said. "He kissed me."   810
"Kissed you?" "Yes, as I said,

But completely against my will."
"No: with your knowledge—and you liked it.
I see no signs that you fought him,"
He declared, bitten by jealousy.   815
"Do you think I don't know you?
Oh yes—how well I know you!
My eyes aren't so weak
That I can't see you're lying.
You're on a dangerous road,   820
Full of pain and unpleasantness;
Your horse won't swallow a grain
Of oats or sleep in a barn
Till I've been avenged—and when
He throws a shoe, by God!   825
He can limp along without it.
If he dies, you'll follow along
Behind me on foot, and you'll never
Get to change your clothes—
No! you'll follow on foot,   830
And naked, till I cut off his head:
That's the only justice I want."
Then he sat himself down and ate.
     And the boy went galloping on
Till he saw a charcoal-maker   835
Pushing a donkey down the road.
"You there," he said, "pushing
A donkey down the road:
Tell me the way to Carlisle.
I want to visit King Arthur   840
And be made a knight: they say
He does that." "My boy, over there's
A castle built on the shore.

Good friend, you'll find King Arthur
In that castle, happy and sad,   845
If that's where you go looking."
"But tell me, please, why
King Arthur is happy and sad."
"I'll tell you the whole story.
King Arthur and all his men   850
Have been fighting with King Ryon.
That king of the Islands was defeated,
And that's why Arthur is happy.
Then all his barons went home,
Back to their own castles,   855
Where they live a better life,
And he doesn't know what they're up to,
And that's why the king is sad."
The boy paid no attention
To anything the fellow said,   860
Except to follow the road
To the king, in the direction shown him,
And coming to the sea he saw
A well-built, beautiful castle,
And riding out from its gate   865
Was a knight in armor, carrying
A golden cup in his hand:
The knight's lance, and his reins,
And his shield, were all in his left hand;
The golden cup in his right,   870
And his armor suited him beautifully,
All of it colored bright red.
And seeing this lovely armor,
Gleaming completely new,
The boy was delighted: "Oh Lord,   875

That's what I'll ask the king
To give me! How happy I'll be,
If he does; I'll never seek
Another!" He was hurrying to the castle,
Anxious to reach Arthur's court,   880
And was riding by the knight
In red, when that knight stopped him:
"Where are you hurrying, boy?"
"I'm heading to court," was the answer,
"To ask the king for armor   885
And weapons." "Go quickly, and come back,
And be sure to tell that worthless
King he'll hold his lands
Subject to me, or else
He'll either give them to me   890
Or send someone to defend them
Against me, for I declare
They all belong to me.
And tell him, so he knows you're telling
The truth, that I took this cup   895
Out of his hand, just now,
As he was drinking his wine."
He should have sought another
Messenger, for nothing he said
Got through. The boy rode straight   900
To the court, where the king and all
His knights were sitting at table.
The hall was at ground-floor level,
As long as it was wide
And paved with stone, so the boy   905
Came riding right in on his horse.
Seated at the head of a table,

King Arthur was deep in thought;
His knights were chattering away,
Laughing and amusing themselves,   910
While he sat lost and mute.
The boy went clopping along,
Not knowing where to find
The king, or whom to address,
Till he happened on a page named Yonet,   915
Standing with a knife in his hand.
"Young fellow," said the boy. "You—
With the knife in your hand—show me
Which of these men is the king."
And Yonet, who was always polite,   920
Answered, "My friend, over there."
So the boy rode to the king,
Whom he greeted in his usual way.
But the king said nothing, sat silent
And still. And the boy spoke   925
Once more, but the king stayed silent.
"By God!" the boy exclaimed,
"This king hasn't made any knights!
How could he create knights
If he never says a word?"   930
So he started to make his way back,
Swinging his horse's head
Around, but like a clumsy
Oaf let the animal
Come too close—it's the truth!—   935
And knocked the king's silk hat
Onto the table. The king
Lifted his lowered head
And looking up at the boy

Put aside his thoughts   940
And said, "Welcome, good sir.
Forgive me: don't take it as rudeness,
Please, that I failed to acknowledge
Your greeting. Sadness kept me
From speaking, for my very worst enemy,   945
The man I hate and fear
The most, came here and claimed
My lands, and he's wild enough
To try to take them away.
He's called the Red Knight,   950
And he comes from the Forest of Quincroy.
And the queen was sitting across
From me, right at this table,
Comforting wounded knights
With kind words and her royal presence.   955
I wouldn't have minded this knight,
Regardless of what he said,
But he grabbed the cup from in front of me
And raised it with so sudden a motion
That he spilled it—it was filled to the brim—   960
All over the queen, which was such
A shameful, disgusting insult
That the queen immediately left,
Angry and upset enough
To kill herself, and she's locked   965
In her room, and whether she'll emerge
Alive, as God is my witness,
I don't know." The king's story
Couldn't have meant less to the boy,
And the queen's sorrow and shame   970
Meant exactly as much. "My lord

King," he said, "make me
A knight, for I'm anxious to leave."
The young savage's eyes
Were exceedingly merry and clear;   975
No one watching could think him
Polite, but all could see
He was handsome and of noble birth.
"My friend," said the king, "dismount,
And let this page hold   980
Your horse; he'll care for it well,
And I swear, as God is my witness,
I'll do as you wish, as both
My honor and yours require."
But the boy replied, "The knights   985
I met, back home, never
Came down from their horses, and yet
You want me to dismount! No,
By God, I won't dismount:
Just get it done, and I'll leave!"   990
"Ah!" said the king. "Dear friend,
I'll gladly do as you wish,
As the honor of us both requires."
"My lord the king," said the boy,
"By the faith I owe to my Maker,   995
I won't be a knight at all
If I can't be a knight in red.
Give me the weapons and armor
Of the knight I met at your door,
With your golden cup in his hand."   1000
     Sir Kay, deeply offended
By all he'd heard, grew angry
And said, "You're right, my friend.

Hurry: go take those weapons
And that armor. They belong to you.   1005
You've done exactly right,
Coming here to claim them."
"Kay," said the king, "by God,
You speak hurtful words
And never worry who's hurt!   1010
That's the very worst vice, in a knight.
This boy is foolish and untaught,
But he may have been born to a noble
Family, and if education's
The problem, perhaps he's had   1015
A bad teacher, and can still improve.
It's sinful to mock and make fun,
And promise what isn't yours
To give. No honest knight
Should ever promise anything   1020
He can't or won't want to give,
For he'll end by making enemies
Of the friends to whom he's made promises:
They'll want what he's said they can have
And are angry not to have it.   1025
Let this teach you: it's better
To refuse a man from the start
Than lead him on with promises.
To tell the simple truth,
The man who says he will—   1030
But won't—is only deceiving
Himself, for he loses a friend."
          And as the king was speaking
The boy was about to leave,
But saw a beautiful, noble   1035

Girl, and stopped to greet her;
Returning his greeting, she began
To laugh and, laughing, said,
"If you live long enough, boy,
I think, and my heart believes,   1040
There'll be no better knight
In this world than you: no one
Will ever see or know
A better one. And that's what I think."
And this was a girl who hadn't   1045
Laughed for more than six years,
And she spoke so loud and clear
That everyone heard her. But her words
Angered Kay, who jumped up
And, slapping her tender face   1050
Hard, with his open palm,
Stretched her out on the ground.
And then, returning to his seat,
He saw a court fool
Standing beside a fireplace   1055
And furiously kicked him into
The blazing flames, for this fool
Had often declared, like a prophet,
"Don't ever expect
This girl to laugh until   1060
She sees the man fated
To become the knight of all knights."
The girl wept, and the fool
Cried, but the boy wouldn't stop,
Asking no one's leave   1065
As he chased the Red Knight.
And Yonet, master of the roads

In all directions, anxious
To carry news to the court,
Left his friends and ran   1070
Across the orchard outside
The hall and through a back gate
Till he reached the road the Red Knight
Had taken, awaiting whatever
Noble adventure might come   1075
His way. And the boy came galloping
Toward the knight whose armor
And weapons he wanted, and the knight
Awaited him (having set the golden
Cup on a slab of gray rock).   1080
As soon as the boy was close
Enough to be heard, he shouted,
"Set that nice red armor
On the ground; it's no longer yours.
This is King Arthur's order!"   1085
And the knight inquired, "Fellow,
Is there anyone here who dares
Uphold the king? If there is,
Just say so: don't try to hide it."
"The devil! What's this? Are you mocking   1090
Me, Sir Knight, not taking
Off my armor? Now hurry
Up and do it. That's an order!"
"Fellow," said the knight, "I asked you
If anyone here wanted   1095
To fight me in the king's name."
"Knight, take off that armor
At once, or I'll take it off you
Myself. I won't wait all day.

Understand me. I'll hit you,   1100
By God, if you keep on gabbing."
At this the knight grew angry
And, raising his lance in both hands,
Hit the boy across
The shoulder with the wooden part,   1105
Striking as hard as he could
And knocking the boy flat
Against his horse's neck.
And the boy, feeling himself
Wounded by the savage blow   1110
He'd received, was furious. Aiming
Straight for the other's eye,
He threw his sharpened stick,
And before the Red Knight knew
What was happening, the stick went through   1115
His eye to his brain, and blood
And brains poured down his neck.
The shock stopped his heart
And he fell backward, dead.
And the boy dismounted, set   1120
The lance aside and lifted
The shield from the dead man's neck,
But couldn't get the helmet
Off, not knowing how
It was fastened on. And he would have been   1125
Happy to take the dead knight's
Sword, but had no idea
How to draw it out,
And stood there, pulling at the scabbard.
And seeing how clumsy he was,   1130
Yonet began to laugh:

"What's going on, my friend?
What are you doing?" "I don't know.
I thought your king gave me
All these weapons and armor,   1135
But I'd have to slice this corpse
Into bite-size bits before
I could get at anything he's got:
Inside and out, all of it
Sticks to him so hard   1140
It's as if this knight and his armor
Were all one solid piece."
"You're all upset about nothing,"
Said Yonet. "I can easily take it
Off, if you like." "Then do it   1145
And do it quickly," said the boy,
"I can't wait any longer!"
Yonet promptly stripped
The corpse from head to toe.
The body was left with no mail shirt   1150
Or stockings, no helmet on its head—
Nothing. But the boy refused
To give up his own clothing,
And nothing Yonet could say
Would make him accept a silk   1155
Coat, beautifully padded
To absorb blows (the knight
Had worn it under his mail shirt),
Or remove the clumsy rawhide
Shoes from his feet. "Damn it!"   1160
Said the boy. "You've got to be joking.
You think I'll exchange the good
Clothes my mother made me

For the stuff this knight was wearing?
Give up my good strong hempen   1165
Shirt for that flimsy thing
He wore under his armor?
Trade my coat that keeps out
The rain for that one, which couldn't
Stop a drop? Damn   1170
The man who'll trade good clothes
For bad! He deserves to rot!"
But how do you teach a fool?
All he'd take was the weapons
And armor; no words could move him.   1175
So Yonet laced up the leggings
And fitted the spurs over
His thick rawhide shoes,
Then took the mail shirt, the best
Ever made, and put it   1180
On him, and set the helmet
On his head (it fitted perfectly),
Then showed him how to hang
The sword loosely on his belt.
Then he put the boy's foot   1185
In the stirrup and helped him mount
The war horse, for the boy had never
In his life used stirrups or spurs,
But only whips and switches.
Then Yonet brought the shield   1190
And spear, and handed them over.
But before he rode off, the boy
Declared, "My friend, take
My horse, lead him away.
He's very good, and now   1195

I don't need him, so I give him to you.
And bring this cup to the king
And greet him in my name. And tell
The girl—the one that Kay
Slapped in the face—that before   1200
I die, if I can, I'll cook up
Something to make him dance
And give her a decent revenge."
Yonet replied that he'd carry
The cup to the king and carefully   1205
Transmit the message he'd been given.
    They went their separate ways.
Yonet returned to the great
Hall where the barons were
And gave the king his cup,   1210
Saying, "Rejoice, my lord,
For your knight, who was here just now,
Has sent you back your cup."
"What knight are you talking about?"
Demanded the king, still burning   1215
With anger. "In the name of God,
My lord, the boy who came
And left not long ago."
"Do you mean that Welsh fellow,"
The king replied, "who wanted   1220
The bright red armor worn
By that knight who brings me shame
As often and as badly as he can?"
"My lord, yes, it's him."
"And how did he get my cup?   1225
Is the Red Knight such a good friend
That he lovingly handed it over?"

"Ah, no. The boy made him
Pay with his life. He killed him."
"My friend: how did he do it?"   1230
"I don't know, my lord, but I saw it:
The knight hit him with his spear
And hurt him badly, and the boy
Returned the favor, hurling
One of his wooden sticks   1235
Through the knight's eye, so blood
And brains spilled from the back
Of his head, and he fell to the ground,
Dead." "Oh steward!" said the king
To Sir Kay, "You've done me a terrible   1240
Wrong! Your bitter tongue—
The cause of so much trouble—
Has now deprived me of this young
Man, who's helped me so much!"
"My lord," Yonet went on,   1245
"He also ordered me
To tell the queen's young maid,
The one Kay hurt—
Slapping her for pure spite—
That if he lived he'd revenge her   1250
If he ever had the chance."
Hearing this, the delighted
Fool (who was near the fire)
Came jumping and running to the king,
Leaping and dancing for joy: 1255
"Great king, as God is my Savior
Now we'll have adventures!
They're going to be savage and hard,
As you'll soon see for yourself,

And I promise you this: Kay   1260
Is going to be sorry for what
His hands and his feet and his foolish,
Villainous tongue have done,
And before a week's gone by
That knight will take revenge   1265
For the kick I got from Kay's foot
And the violent slap in the face
He gave the queen's young maid—
Ah, how your steward will pay!
He's going to break his right arm   1270
Between the elbow and the armpit,
And he'll carry it around in a sling
For half a year—oh yes
He will, it's as certain as death!"
These words were so painful to Kay   1275
That he felt as if he would burst
With anger, so furious that he almost—
Right in front of them all—
Struck the fool dead
On the spot. But knowing he'd displease   1280
The king, he stopped himself
In time. And the king said, "Ah!
Sir Kay, what trouble you've caused me!
If only we'd taken this boy
In hand, and helped him learn   1285
What weapons and armor were for—
The proper use of spears
And shields—he'd already be a knight,
And a good one. But he knows nothing
Of knighthood, or anything else,   1290
And couldn't so much as unsheathe

His sword, if he had to. And there
He is, armed and mounted
On a war horse, and he'll meet some rascal
Who wants that horse and will handle him   1295
Roughly to get it. Indeed,
Unable to defend himself,
Foolish, completely untaught,
He'll soon be wounded, or dead.
You'll see, it won't take long!"   1300
      Thus the king lamented,
His face showing his sadness,
But knowing how helpless he was
He said nothing more.
Meanwhile, the boy was spurring   1305
His horse straight through the forest,
Emerging at the edge of a plain
Bordered by a river swelled
By water from all around,
And broader across than a crossbow   1310
Could shoot over. He rode down
To the bank of this mighty stream,
But was careful not to ride
Into the water, for he saw
It was deeper and blacker and ran   1315
Even faster than the Loire.
So he rode along the bank,
Where the swift-flowing water beat
Against the base of a massive
Cliff. And just at the point   1320
Where the rock sloped to the river,
Stood a rich and powerful castle.
Where the water went pouring into

A bay, the boy turned left
And saw the castle towers   1325
(Or so it seemed to him)
Springing directly out
Of the rock as he watched. And right
In the center of the castle soared
The tallest tower of all.   1330
A strongly built gate
Faced the bay, completely
Barring the path up
From the water, which lapped at its feet.
In the four corners of the surrounding   1335
Wall (fashioned of quarried
Rocks) were four low
Towers, beautifully shaped
And strong. The location was perfect,
The whole castle built   1340
For comfort. In front of the round
Gatehouse, the moat was spanned
By a bridge of cemented stone,
Tall and strong, with battle
Stations set along   1345
Its length, and a tower in the middle,
With a drawbridge in front, well
Constructed to serve its purpose—
A bridge for daytime hours,
But a gate at night. The boy   1350
Proceeded to the bridge, on which
A distinguished man in ermine
Robes had been walking; he was waiting,
Now, for the horseman coming
Toward him. As a sign of his stature   1355

And importance, he held a baton
In his hand; two pages (in simple
Garments, not wearing their cloaks)
Were standing close behind him.
Keeping his mother's lessons   1360
In mind, the boy called out,
Politely, as he came closer,
"Good sir, as my mother taught me
To say, God's blessings on you,
Brother." And the nobleman addressed him,   1365
Seeing what a simpleton he was:
"Brother, where have you come from?"
"Where? King Arthur's court."
"And why?" "The king, may he have
Good fortune, made me a knight."   1370
"A knight? May God protect me,
I wouldn't have thought he had time,
Right now, to give to such things.
It seemed to me he'd have
Too much else on his mind.   1375
But tell me, please, good brother,
Where did you get your armor?"
"I got it as a gift from the king."
"A gift? Tell me about it."
And the boy told the story   1380
You've been hearing. To tell it
Again would be stupid and boring:
Who wants a twice-told tale?
Then the nobleman asked him if he knew
How to manage his horse.   1385
"I can make him run up and down,
Just like the hunting horse

I used to have, the one
I took from my mother's house."
"And your armor, good friend: tell me   1390
If you know how it works?" "I know
How to put it on, and take it
Off, as a page showed me,
Because I watched him taking it
Off the dead knight who'd worn it,   1395
And believe me it's all so light
It isn't hard to wear."
"I'm pleased to hear it," said the nobleman,
"Truly delighted. But tell me,
Please, if you have no objection,   1400
What has brought you here?"
"Sir, my mother taught me
To look for brave and noble
Men who could give me good
Advice, and to listen to their words,   1405
For belief in them is well placed."
And the nobleman answered, "Friend,
May your mother be blessed, for the counsel
She gave you is splendid. But isn't there
Anything else you want?"   1410
"Yes." "What?" "Only
This: to give me lodging
Tonight." "Gladly," said the nobleman,
"But grant me, first, a request
Which will do you a world of good."   1415
"What is it you want?" "Follow
Your mother's advice, and trust me."
"By God," said the boy, "I'll do that."
"Then dismount from your horse." And he did.

One of the pages who'd come   1420
With the nobleman took the boy's horse,
And the other took off his armor.
And there he stood, in the stupid
Garments he'd had from his mother,
Clodhopper boots and rawhide   1425
Coat, clumsily sewn.
And then the nobleman put on
The sharp steel spurs that the boy
Had brought with him, and mounted
The boy's horse, and hung   1430
The shield by its strap around
His neck, and took up the spear,
And said, "My friend, it's time
To learn how these weapons are managed.
Observe how this spear is held   1435
And the horse is spurred forward, then checked."
He untied the banner wrapped
Around the spear, then taught
The boy how the shield was used.
He lowered it down until   1440
It almost touched the horse's
Neck, then set the spear
At rest, then spurred the splendid
Horse, which responded at once,
Obeying every command.   1445
And the nobleman had profound knowledge
Of horses and shields and spears;
He'd studied these arts from his childhood.
The boy was thrilled, watching
What the nobleman could do. And when   1450
The dazzling performance was finished

(The boy hanging on every
Move), the nobleman came riding
Back, the spear held high
In the air, and asked the boy,   1455
"My friend, would you care to take
A turn, handling spear
And shield and working the horse?"
And the boy's eager answer
Assured him he'd rather not live   1460
A single day longer, or own
An acre of land, until
He could do as much. "My friend,
One can learn what one does not know,
Provided one works at learning.   1465
Every craft requires
Clear eyes, and effort, and heart:
These three conditions are all
One needs. But since you know
Nothing, and have seen nothing,   1470
Decide, if you will, to learn
Nothing, and no one will blame you."
        Then the nobleman had him mount
And, the moment he started, the boy
Began to handle shield   1475
And spear as if he'd spent
His life winning tournaments
And wars, traveling all over
The world, seeking adventure—
For to him the arts of battle   1480
Were second nature, and when
The teacher is Nature, and the student's
Heart is at home, learning's

Not hard, for Nature and heart
Work together. With this double help   1485
He did wonderfully well, and the happy
Nobleman said to himself
That had the boy been working
Since birth he'd now be exactly
The master he'd suddenly become.   1490
Having completed his practice,
The boy came riding back,
Lance held high (as he'd seen
The nobleman hold it), and asked,
"Sir, did I do it right?   1495
Do you think I'd have a chance
Of succeeding, if I tried very hard?
In all my life I've never
Seen a thing I wanted
So much. I long to master   1500
These arts as you have done."
"My friend," was the answer, "if you have
The heart you'll learn what you need to:
Don't torture yourself with doubt."
     Three times the nobleman mounted   1505
The horse, and showed the boy
The things he needed to know,
And then three times the boy
Took his turn in the saddle.
And after the third time the nobleman   1510
Asked, "My friend, if you meet
A knight, what will you do
If he strikes you?" "I'll strike him back."
"And what if your spear shatters?"
"What else could I do? I'll hit   1515

Him hard, with both my fists."
"And that will accomplish nothing."
"Then what should I do?" "You'll need
To attack him, sword in hand."
The nobleman planted his spear   1520
Straight up and down in the ground,
Deeply concerned to teach
The boy all that a man
Should know about using his sword,
When the time came, either   1525
Defending himself or attacking.
So he took his sword in hand:
"My friend, if you're attacked,
Here's the way to defend
Yourself." "God save me!" said the boy.   1530
"I know all that as well
As anyone. I practiced until
I dropped, on pillows and padded
Shields, at my mother's house."
"Then come take lodgings with me,"   1535
Said his host. "There's nothing more
To do. No matter what anyone
Thinks, tonight we'll lodge
You well." They walked together,
Side by side. "Sir,"   1540
Said the boy, "my mother taught me
Never to spend much time
With any man unless
I knew his name. This seems
To me exactly right,   1545
So I'd like to know your name."
"Good friend," the nobleman said,

"I'm Gornemant de Goort."
And so they came to the house,
Walking hand in hand.   1550
And as they ascended the steps
A page came running up,
Carrying a short cloak,
And hurriedly draped it around
The boy, to keep him from catching   1555
Cold, all heated from exertion
As he was. The house was large,
Beautiful, and rich, the servants
Excellent, and the food they'd prepared
Was fine and perfectly served.   1560
The knights first washed their hands,
Then seated themselves at table,
The nobleman sitting next
To the boy, and eating with him
From the very same bowl. No one   1565
Needs to know just what
They ate, exactly what dishes:
They dined, and they drank, till they stopped,
And that's all I'll say on the subject.
          And when they rose from the table   1570
The careful, courteous host
Asked the boy who'd been sitting
Beside him to be his guest
For a month. Or a year, if he cared to,
For by keeping him there the host   1575
Could continue teaching him things —
If he thought them pleasant to learn —
He'd some day be glad he knew.
But the boy answered, "Sir,

Whether I'm near my mother's   1580
House I have no idea,
But I hope that God on high
Will lead me there and let me
See her again, for I saw her
Faint near the bridge at her door.   1585
Is she living? Is she dead? I don't know.
She fainted from sadness, because
I was leaving, I know she did,
And so I find it impossible
To linger long anywhere   1590
Else, until I know
How she is. I'll be leaving at dawn."
The nobleman knew that nothing
Would change his mind, and said
Nothing. Their beds were made,   1595
And without a word they went to them.
  Next morning, the nobleman rose
And came to the boy's bed
(In which he found him still lying)
Carrying, as farewell gifts,   1600
A linen shirt and pants,
And shoes dyed fiery red,
And a coat made in India
And sewn of Indian silk.
These were presents he meant   1605
The boy to wear, so he said,
"My friend, if you trust my words,
Put on these clothes." And the boy
Replied, "Good sir, you could
Have spoken kinder words.   1610
Aren't the clothes my mother

Made me better than these?
But you want me to put these on!"
"Young man," said the host, "I swear
You promised you'd take my advice   1615
And do whatever I said
You should do. You did, my friend,
You did. So do as I ask you."
"Gladly," was the answer, "for I've no
"Desire to disobey you   1620
In any way whatever."
And with no further delay
He dressed in the new clothes and abandoned
The old. And then the nobleman
Bent and affixed a spur   1625
To the boy's right foot: a knight
Creating another knight
Is expected to attach this spur.
And then a host of pages
Set themselves to properly   1630
Arming the new young knight.
Then the nobleman took up the sword,
Belted it on the boy,
And kissed him, saying that thus
He conferred the highest distinction   1635
God had ever created,
The order of knighthood; knights,
He declared, were sworn to honor.
And he added, "Brother, remember:
Whenever you engage in combat   1640
With another knight, do
Exactly as I now instruct you.
If you gain the upper hand,

And the other cannot defend
Himself or continue the battle,   1645
And is forced to beg for mercy,
Don't deliberately kill him.
Nor should you let yourself
Talk too much, or gossip.
Whoever talks too much   1650
Is sure to say something
That someone will find offensive.
Wise men declare, over
And over, 'Too much talking
Is sinful.' And so, good brother,   1655
I warn you, be careful. And I urge you,
If you find a girl or a woman,
Unmarried or married, deprived
Of assistance and counsel, provide it:
Women deserve our help,   1660
If we know what ought to be done
And are able, ourselves, to do it.
         "And let me also teach you
This: listen well;
These words are worth your attention.   1665
Remember to go to church
And pray to the Maker of us all
To bless your soul with His mercy
And, here in this worldly life,
Protect you as the Christian you are."   1670
To which the boy answered,
"May you be blessed, good sir,
By all the apostles of Rome,
For you say what my mother said."
"Please, good brother," the nobleman   1675

Said, "don't explain
That your mother told you this
Or that. I'm not offended,
Hearing such things. But others,
If you keep announcing the fact   1680
(Which is why I beg you never
To say it again!), are sure
To take you for an absolute fool.
Please: do try to be careful."
"What then should I say, good sir?"   1685
"You can always say that the man
Who gave you your spur told you
These things, and taught you well."
And the boy promised he'd never
Say a single word,   1690
The rest of his life, of the lessons
He'd learned, except to declare
That his host had been his best teacher.
And the nobleman raised his hand
Above the boy's head, and blessed him,   1695
Saying, "Good sir, God save you!
As long as you won't stay here,
Go with God, who will lead you."
          So the new-made knight left
His host, worried he'd taken   1700
Too long to return to his mother
And assure himself she was well
And alive. He rode through the lonely
Forests, feeling more at home
In the woods than the flat plains,   1705
Riding until he came
To a great castle, well

Located but surrounded by the sea
And the waves and desolate fields.
He rode rapidly toward   1710
The castle and soon reached the gate,
But saw he'd first need to cross
A bridge so weak and worn
He had some doubt it would hold him.
He started across, and it neither   1715
Did him harm nor caused him
Shame, but took him safely
Over. He went right to the gate,
And found it closed and locked,
So he knocked and called for admittance   1720
(Not afraid to raise his voice
And demand that someone come)
Until a wan and wasted-
Looking girl appeared
At a window: "Who's that out there?"   1725
She said. He looked up at the window,
Saw her, and said, "My lovely
Friend, I'm a knight who's come here
To ask that you let me in
And offer me lodging for the night."   1730
"Good sir," she replied, "you shall have it,
But you won't be pleased that you did.
Yet nevertheless we'll give you
What hospitality we can."
        When the girl had gone away   1735
The knight, watching and waiting
At the gate, was afraid he'd be staying there
And began to bang once more,
And soon four soldiers came,

Great axes hung from their necks   1740
And each with a sword at his belt,
And they quickly opened the gate,
Saying, "Sir, come in."
They might have been first-rate soldiers,
Once, but had suffered so much   1745
Privation, both in youth and in age,
That seeing their state no one
Could help but marvel. Everything
Outside was ruined and wasted,
Bare and stark, but inside   1750
Nothing was any better,
And everywhere one went
Were empty, deserted streets
And abandoned houses, falling
To pieces, no men, no women   1755
To be seen. The town had had
Two churches, housing two
Religious orders, but the monks
Had been frightened away, and the nuns
Had fled. Those churches were neither   1760
Rich nor lovely, their walls
Full of cracks and falling
Apart, their towers roofless,
Their doors hanging open
And unlocked both night and day.   1765
Nowhere in all the town
Was a mill grinding or an oven
Lit—no bread and no biscuits,
Nor nothing worth so much
As a penny anywhere for sale.   1770
        The town had become a wasteland,

With nothing to eat, no wine
Or cider or beer to drink.
Taking their visitor to a slate-
Roofed hall, the four soldiers   1775
Helped him dismount and take off
His armor. And then a page
Came down the stairs, bearing
A cloak trimmed with gray fur;
He draped it around the knight's neck,   1780
While others led his horse
To a stable that offered little
Fodder or grain, having
Almost none to give.
And others conducted the visitor   1785
Up the stairs and into
The main hall, which was lovely,
And where two noble knights
And a girl were waiting to receive him.
Both knights were gray-haired, though their heads 1790
Were not yet totally silvered.
They would have been in the prime
Of life, had they not been oppressed
And wearied by troubles and cares.
But the girl walked more lightly,   1795
Obviously elegant, more graceful
Than a singing bird or a hawk.
Her cloak and her gown were a deep,
Rich black silk studded
With gold, and both were bordered   1800
With thick, perfect ermine.
Her cloak was hemmed with black
And silver sable, neither

Particularly long nor wide.
Whatever descriptions I've given   1805
Of a beautiful woman's face
And body, blessed by God,
I'd like to attempt again,
And this once in perfect truth.
Her head was bare, and her hair—   1810
Hard as it is to believe—
Glowed so clear and bright
It almost seemed to be spun
Of the finest gold. Her forehead
Was high, pale and smooth   1815
As if polished by the careful hand
Of a sculptor, who'd carved her face
In marble or ivory. Her eyebrows
Were brown, set well apart,
And her eyes, brilliant, piercing,   1820
Were wide and clear and gay.
Her nose was straight, but not short,
And tints of crimson and white
Showed better, across her face,
Than bright red cloth laid   1825
On silver. God made her surpassingly
Lovely to disorder men's minds
And hearts, and having shaped
One such marvel never
Made another like her.   1830
She and the knights who were with her
Greeted the knight, and he them,
And then the young woman cheerfully
Took him by the hand, and said,
"Good brother, I'm afraid your lodgings,   1835

Tonight, won't be as good
As noble knights are used to.
But if I tell you, now,
Exactly how we live,
You're likely to think we told you   1840
Only for wicked reasons,
To be rid of your presence. But please,
Accept the hospitality
We're able to offer: tomorrow
May God provide you with better!"   1845
Still holding him by the hand
She led him to a secret room,
Long and broad and beautiful,
And seated herself beside him
On a silk-covered feather-quilt   1850
Laid out across a bed.
Groups of knights, four
And five and six at a time,
Came in and silently seated
Themselves, watching the new   1855
Young knight sitting next
To their lady, and equally silent,
Remembering the warning his noble
Teacher had given him. But among
Themselves, in whispers, the lady's   1860
Knights had a great deal to say:
"Good lord," they said, "I wonder
If this knight can talk at all.
What a shame that would be: no better-
Looking knight has ever   1865
Been born. He looks good with our lady,
And she looks good with him.

He's so handsome and she
So lovely that, if only they weren't
So silent, no girl and no knight   1870
Could go better, one with the other,
Than these two, side by side—
As if God had expressly made them
So He could join them together."
And everyone there had something   1875
To say on this subject, while the girl
Waited patiently for him
To begin their conversation,
And finally saw quite clearly
That nothing could make him open   1880
His mouth until she had spoken,
So she said, with perfect courtesy,
"My lord, where have you come from?"
"Young lady," he said, "my lodgings
Last night were at a nobleman's   1885
Castle, and they were good ones.
The castle had five strong towers—
One big one, and four that were small.
I can't describe it fully,
Nor even tell you its name,   1890
But I know quite well the nobleman's
Name is Gornemant of Goort."
"Ah, my friend!" said the girl,
"How well you've spoken—exactly
The words of a courteous knight.   1895
Our Lord in Heaven must be pleased
At what you've said of Gornemant.
You couldn't have spoken more truly,
For by Saint Riquier he's noble

Indeed, as I can bear witness: 1900
I haven't seen him in a very
Long time, but I'm his niece,
So I know that since you left him
You can't have met with a man
More noble. And I'm also sure   1905
He rejoiced to find himself
Your host, for he welcomes guests
As a courteous nobleman should,
Secure in his wealth and power.
But here we've only six loaves   1910
Of bread, sent me, along
With a cask of reheated wine,
By another of my uncles, a saintly
Priest, to have something for supper.
We've nothing else to eat   1915
Except a deer that one
Of my men killed with an arrow."
And then she ordered tables
Set up, and they were, and they all
Sat down to eat their meal.   1920
        It did not take them long,
But they relished whatever there was.
And then those who'd been
On watch, the night before,
Stayed in the hall to sleep,   1925
And those who were standing guard
That night went out and assumed
Their posts. Fifty knights
And pages kept the watch,
While those who remained labored   1930
To make their guest comfortable.

Those in charge of his bed
Made it with beautiful linen
And costly coverlets and pillows,
And everything else they could think of   1935
To make their guest as happy
As possible that night, excepting
Only the pleasure a pretty
Girl might have supplied,
Or a lady, if he'd let them provide one.   1940
But the boy knew nothing of such things
And fell asleep, I can tell you,
As soon as he lay himself down,
For his mind was completely untroubled.
But his hostess, shut in her room,   1945
Could neither rest nor sleep.
He slept like a log, but she lay there
Thinking, unable to defend
Herself in the battle she was fighting.
She turned this way and that,   1950
Too tormented to sleep.
Then draping a short cloak
Of bright red silk over
Her nightshirt, she ventured out
Like the brave and spirited girl   1955
She was—but not on some silly,
Selfish quest, but intending
To seek out her guest and tell him
Some part of the problems she faced.
Still, when she'd left her bed   1960
And ventured out of her room
She shook in every limb,
And fear pounded in her heart.

She passed through the door in tears,
And when she reached his bed   1965
She stood there, weeping and sighing.
And then she knelt, bending
Over him, the tears flowing
So freely that they covered his face:
She could manage nothing more.   1970
   The flood of tears woke him,
Startled, wondering why
His face was covered with water.
And then he saw her kneeling
Next to his bed, and felt her   1975
Clutching him round the neck.
Politely wrapping his arms
Around her, he gently drew her
Down, saying, as he did so,
"What is it you wish, beautiful   1980
Lady? Why are you here?"
"Oh noble knight, have mercy!
I pray you by God and His son,
Don't change your opinion of me
Because I've come to your bed.   1985
Don't think me wild and foolish
And wicked because I'm wearing
Only my nightshirt, for in all
This world there's no one afflicted
With misery and sadness whose pain   1990
And suffering can equal mine.
I no longer want anything;
Despair is all my days
Bring me. I'm so lost in sadness
That this will be the final   1995

Night of my life and tomorrow
My very last day, for I mean
To kill myself. Once
This castle was guarded by more
Than three hundred knights. Fifty   2000
Are left: the rest—two hundred
Men and more—have been taken
Away, imprisoned or killed
By Anguinguerron, steward
Of Clamadeu of the Islands,   2005
And the very worst man alive.
The fate of those he's imprisoned
Hurts me as sorely as those
He's killed: they're as good as dead,
They'll never be seen again.   2010
With so many brave men dead
For me, no wonder I'm distraught!
          "They besieged this castle all winter
Long, and all summer long:
Anguinguerron wouldn't budge.   · 2015
His army grew larger and larger,
While ours kept getting smaller,
And our stores of food kept shrinking,
Until we hadn't enough
To feed a hungry bee!   2020
We've sunk so low that nothing
Less than God Himself
Can save us: tomorrow this castle,
Which can't be defended, will fall,
And I'd be a prisoner, too—   2025
If I let them take me alive,
Which I won't. I'll kill myself first,

And then I don't care if they take me.
Clamadeu wants me, and thinks
He'll have me—but never living—   2030
Only dead in both body
And soul. I've hidden a knife
Of the finest steel in my jewel box
And I'll plunge it into my heart.
And that's what I had to tell you.   2035
So now I'll go away
And let you go back to sleep."
          Ah, what an opportunity
For glory, if he's brave enough
To seize it. And that's what she came for,   2040
Dropping her tears on his face,
In spite of the story she'd told him.
She'd come for that and nothing
Else, hoping, if he had
The courage, he'd decide to fight   2045
For her castle, and her lands, and for her.
And he said, "My dear sweet friend,
Let yourself smile, be comforted
Now. And no more crying:
Just lie down here with me,   2050
And wipe those tears from your eyes.
God in His goodness may bring you
Better tidings, tomorrow.
Stretch out here on this bed:
There's plenty of room for us both.   2055
I promise not to forsake you."
"If that's what you want," she said,
"That's what I'll do." And as
He held her in his arms, he kissed her.

With infinite care he covered her   2060
With his blanket, as gently as he could,
And she let him kiss her again,
Nor did his kisses displease her.
And then they spent the night
Lying together, mouth   2065
To mouth, till morning came.
            That night she knew the pleasures
Of sleeping in each other's arms,
Mouth to mouth, until dawn.
And when morning came the girl   2070
Went back to her room, walking
Alone, and dressed herself,
That day, with no chambermaid's help,
Careful to awaken no one.
And when those who'd spent the night   2075
On guard saw daylight breaking
They woke up those who'd slept,
And the sleepers quickly rose
From their beds and made themselves ready.
And then the girl hurried   2080
Back to her knight and gave him
A gracious greeting, "Good sir,
May God bless you on your way!
I'm well aware you won't
Be staying here long. You've nothing   2085
To gain by lingering here.
You'll leave us, and I won't be angry
Or show the slightest displeasure:
That would be rude, for we've
Not given you the kind   2090
Of comfort you should have had.

But I trust Our Lord will bring you
Better accommodations
And more bread and wine and salt
Than we've been able to offer."   2095
He answered, "Lady, I won't
Be looking for other lodgings
Today, until I've made
Your lands peaceful, if I can.
I won't let your enemy linger,   2100
If I meet him out there. Let nothing
Torment you, now. But if
I succeed in battle, and kill him,
All I'll want from you
Is your love and affection—I need   2105
No other repayment." To which
She responded, slyly, "Sir,
What you've requested is almost
Worthless, a thing of no value.
But if I refused it you'd think me   2110
Proud and haughty, so I've no
Desire to refuse. But don't
Ask me to become your love
Simply because—either
By agreement or law—you then   2115
Can go and die for my sake!
Oh what a waste that would be!
For I see quite plainly that neither
Your age nor your courage are such
That you could possibly stand   2120
Against so famous a knight,
So fierce and strong, as now
Awaits you, outside, for man

To man you're bound to lose."
"Just wait and see," he said,   2125
"For I'm certainly going to fight him,
And nothing you say will stop me."
She'd spoken as if to hold him
Back, though this was a battle
She longed for. How often we hide   2130
What we want, knowing that negative
Words will push a determined
Mind to do even better
What it's long since decided to do.
She played her part wisely,   2135
Making him think she was strongly
Opposed to what he was doing.
And then he called for his weapons
And armor, and they brought them out,
And made him ready, and helped him   2140
Mount on a horse waiting
In the middle of the courtyard, fully
Equipped. Then they opened the gate.
All of them wore the grimmest
Looks, and warned him, "Good sir,   2145
May God be with you, today,
And bring the very worst luck
To Anguinguerron, the steward,
Who's burned and ruined these lands."
They stood there weeping, both women   2150
And men. And then they led him
To the gate, and watched him go out,
Shouting after him, all
Together, "In the name of the one
True Cross, on which God let His Son   2155

Be killed, may you be kept
From danger and death and imprisonment!
May you come back in safety
And pleasure to whatever place
Best pleases and most delights you!"   2160
      Thus everyone prayed. And when those
In the army outside saw him
Coming, they called to their leader,
Who was waiting in front of his tent,
Sure that before night fell   2165
The castle would be his, even
If one of its weary defenders
Tried to face him in combat.
His leg armor was laced; his troops
Were already rejoicing, convinced   2170
The castle was theirs and they'd conquered
The entire country. The moment
Anguinguerron saw him, he took up
His weapons and hurried to meet him,
Riding hard on a huge   2175
And powerful horse, crying,
"Fellow, who sent you here?
Tell me why you've come:
Is it peace you're after, or a fight?"
"And what are you doing here?"   2180
Was the answer. "First tell me that.
Why have you killed good knights
And ruined this whole land?"
And then the steward replied
With infinite arrogance and pride,   2185
"I want everyone out of
This castle, and the tower surrendered:

I've wasted too much time.
And I want the girl for my lord."
"Damn such stupid words,"   2190
Said the boy, "and whoever speaks them!
There'll be no conquest: you'll have to
Give up your claims, instead."
"Keep your dreams to yourself,"
Said Anguinguerron. "Ah me!   2195
How often the helpless and innocent
Must pay for other people's
Misdeeds!" This arrogance angered
The boy, who set his lance—
And without a challenge or any   2200
More words they charged at each other.
Both had sturdy lances
With sharpened metal points;
Their powerful horses ran hard,
And the knights were strong and angry,   2205
Anxious to kill. As they crashed
Together, their shields and lances
Chipped and cracked, and each
Swept the other to the ground.
But without a word they leapt   2210
Back in their saddles and attacked
More fiercely than a pair of wild boars,
Smashing blows at shields
And iron-linked mail shirts as fast
As their horses could bring them together.   2215
Their arms were so strong, their hearts
So filled with fury, that this time
The lances completely shattered,
Splintered down the middle.

But only Anguinguerron   2220
Fell from his horse, so badly
Wounded that his arm and side
Were extremely painful. Not knowing
How he could fight, now,
Seated high on his horse,   2225
The boy came down to the ground,
Drew his sword, and attacked.
How can I tell you how many
Blows were struck, back
And forth? But the battle lasted   2230
A very long time, and they fought it
Fiercely, until at last
Anguinguerron fell to the ground
And the boy came at him so hard
That he begged for mercy. The boy   2235
Informed him, at once, that mercy
Was completely out of the question.
But then he remembered what his noble
Instructor had taught him: he was not
To deliberately kill in cold blood   2240
Any knight, once the battle
Was over and the man had been conquered.
And Anguinguerron said, "My good friend,
Don't treat me so harshly. I've begged you
For mercy. Grant it. You've taught me   2245
That you're the better knight:
I hereby affirm that fact
And declare you a man of great valor—
But not so well known that anyone
Unfamiliar with your powers   2250
And knowing anything of me

Would believe that, all by yourself,
You could have killed me in battle.
Leave me alive and I'll bear you
Witness that you beat me in combat,   2255
Here in front of my tent
As my army watched, and the world
Will accept my word, and award you
More honor than has ever been known.
And remember: if you serve a lord   2260
For whom you desire a gift
Or to whom you owe a debt,
Just send me to him, and I'll go
As you instruct and say
Precisely how you beat me   2265
In combat, and took me prisoner,
And bound me to do as he
May command."
        "Damned right you will!
And where do you think I'll send you?
Into this castle—and you'll tell   2270
The beautiful girl I love
You'll never bother her
Again, as long as you live,
But place yourself, both body
And soul, completely at her mercy."   2275
The steward answered, "Then kill me,
Because that's just what she'll do.
There's nothing she wants so badly
As torment and death for me:
When her father died, I was there,   2280
And all this past year I drove her
To despair, killing and capturing

So many of her knights. Making
Me her captive is simply
Condemning your prisoner to death.   2285
There's nothing worse you could do.
Isn't there someone else
To whom you could send me, someone
Not so certain to harm me?
There's not a doubt in the world   2290
This girl will kill me."
                    So then
The boy declared he'd send
His prisoner to a nobleman's castle,
And told him the nobleman's name
And—better than any mason—   2295
Described exactly how
That castle was made, in complete
Detail: the moat, the bridge,
And every turret and tower,
And the great walls set around it,   2300
Until the steward knew
That the place he'd go as a captive
Was precisely where he was hated
The most.
                    "Nothing will save me,
Good sir, if you send me there.   2305
As God is my savior, that too
Is a certain route to death.
In the course of this war I killed
One of that lord's own brothers.
Good friend, before you send me   2310
There, I'd rather you killed me
Yourself. Don't send me to my death."

"By God," said the boy, "you'll go
And be King Arthur's captive,
And greet the king in my name,   2315
And tell him, on my behalf,
To show you the girl that Kay,
His steward, struck, when she laughed
At the sight of me, and make
Yourself that girl's prisoner,   2320
And tell her, as soon as you can,
That nothing could possibly make me
Set foot in any court
Held by King Arthur until
I've finally avenged that blow."   2325
And Anguinguerron assured him
He'd do it, and do it well.
Then the victorious knight
Headed back to the castle,
And he who'd been defeated   2330
Rode toward King Arthur's court,
Lifting the siege, lowering
His flags, and leaving no one
Behind him. And the knights of the castle
Rode out to greet their champion,   2335
Their hearts saddened because,
Having conquered the steward,
He hadn't cut off his head
And brought it back in triumph.
But their greeting was joyful. They led him   2340
To a platform and helped him out
Of his armor, saying, "Lord,
Why didn't you cut off his head,
Since you hadn't taken him captive?"

And he replied, "My friends,   2345
That wouldn't have been right, for he'd
Been guilty of killing your kinfolk.
I'd given him my word
And you would have killed him at once.
And what would I be worth   2350
As a knight, refusing him mercy
When I had him down on the ground?
Nor do you know what terms
I gave him: he's pledged himself
A prisoner at King Arthur's court."   2355
Then the mistress of the castle came,
Wonderfully pleased, and led him
Away to her private apartment
To rest and relax. And there
She gave him hugs and kisses,   2360
And denied him nothing at all.
Instead of eating and drinking
They played at hugging and kissing
And murmuring words of endearment.
       But Clamadeu was insanely   2365
Determined. He rode rapidly
Toward the castle, thinking
It conquered. One of his men,
Sad-faced and sorrowing, met him
Along the road, and gave him   2370
The miserable news of his steward.
"By God, it's all gone badly,
My lord!" Half distraught,
He was pulling the hair from his head.
"Just what's gone wrong?" said his lord.   2375
And the man told him, "Your steward's

Been beaten in single combat,
And taken captive, and dispatched
As a prisoner to King Arthur's court."
"But who was able to do this,   2380
And how was it done? Where
On earth could they have found
A knight capable of defeating
So brave, so valiant a man?"
"My beloved lord," was the answer,   2385
"I don't know where he came from,
I can only tell you that I saw him
Riding out of Castle
Beaurepaire, all
In red."
     "And what's to be done?"   2390
Demanded his lord, half out
Of his mind. "What else? Turn
And go home. There's nothing more
To be done. This war is over."
     Hearing these words, a grizzled   2395
Knight came forward. This
Was Clamadeu's master of arms.
"What stupid advice!" he said.
"Our lord requires better
Counsel than this. Following   2400
Your advice would be folly.
Go forward, I say. Go forward!"
And then he went on: "My lord,
Shall I tell you the way to conquer
Both this knight and this castle?   2405
I'll tell you a first-rate plan,
Quick and easy to accomplish.

No one inside this castle's
Walls has eaten or drunk
Very much. They've got to be weak.   2410
But we, we're healthy and strong,
Suffering neither from hunger
Nor thirst. We could fight all day,
If they dared come out against us,
Risk combat hand to hand.   2415
Send twenty knights to their gate
And tempt them into battle.
And the knight, so busy amusing
Himself with Blanchefleur,
His lady, will try to be more   2420
Of a knight than he knows how to be.
Those others are far too feeble
To be of much help, so we'll either
Take him captive or kill him.
But really, all our twenty   2425
Knights need do is keep them
Confused and fighting, while we
Come sneaking through this valley
And fall on them from behind."
"What a grand idea, by God!"   2430
Said Clamadeu. "You're right!
We've got our very best troops—
Five hundred mail-clad knights
And a thousand well-equipped soldiers—
So our enemies are as good as dead."   2435
Then Clamadeu sent twenty
Knights to the castle gate,
In front of which they unfurled
A host of flags and banners,

Fluttering bright in the wind.   2440
And when those in the castle saw them
They flung the gates wide open,
As their new lord had commanded,
And out he came, riding
At their head, to attack their enemies.   2445
Proud and fierce and strong,
He attacked them all at once,
And whoever he struck had no
Illusions about fighting with some weakling
Apprentice. His iron spear   2450
Pierced more than one body!
He struck their guts, and their chests,
He broke their arms and their necks,
Smashing some down, killing
Others. The knights and horses   2455
He captured were handed over
To those on his own side
Who wanted them. Then he saw
A great army approaching,
Five hundred knights coming up   2460
The valley, and a thousand soldiers,
A horde of enemies filling
The fields and heading for the open
Gates. Seeing the slaughter
And destruction wreaked on their ranks,   2465
They ran like wild men, tumbling
One on the other in their haste,
But those defending the gates
Held their ranks, in good
Formation, and fought hard.   2470
But they were few in number, and weak

With hunger, and the enemy had brought up
Every soldier they had,
Making their weight unstoppable;
The defenders retreated to the castle.   2475
Archers posted above
The gates shot arrows into
The mob as it tried to push
And shove its way inside,
And one group got   2480
As far as the entrance. But then
The defenders released a heavy
Hanging gate from above them,
And crashing to the ground it killed
Everyone standing beneath it.   2485
Nothing he'd ever seen
Had so grieved Clamadeu as the sight
Of dozens of his men struck down,
Suddenly crushed to death,
While he could only stand   2490
Outside, helpless, watching
As his hasty, disorganized soldiers
Fell. His grizzled adviser
Consoled him, glibly: "These things
Happen to the bravest, my lord.   2495
If God so wishes it, we know
That—good or bad—we die.
You've lost your men, yes,
And the war with them. But there'll be
A tomorrow! Today's storm   2500
Broke you, our ranks have been thinned
And those inside have won—
But not forever: trust me!

Pluck the eyes from my head
If they last another five days!   2505
This castle and tower will be yours,
And they'll all be your captives, in the end.
Just camp out here today
And tomorrow, and the castle will fall,
And even the girl who's so long   2510
Opposed you will be down on her knees,
Begging in the name of God
That you come and take her prisoner."
So Clamadeu's tent was put up,
Along with the others they'd brought,   2515
While those with no other protection
Took lodgings as best they could.
And the castle's defenders set down
Their weapons. Their own prisoners
Were neither imprisoned nor enchained,   2520
Once they'd pledged on their solemn
Honor as knights to regard
Themselves as captives and to do
No harm to those who had caught them.
        And so they stayed behind   2525
Their walls. That day a great wind
Had blown a heavy barge,
Loaded with wheat and other
Foodstuff, clear out to sea.
God was good enough   2530
To steer it, safe and sound,
To the castle, and when the defenders*

* Lines 1708-9 inform us that the castle is "surrounded by the sea and
the waves"

Saw it, they sent messengers
Down to the shore, to learn
From those on board who   2535
They were and where they'd come from,
What lord they served, and where
They'd been meaning to go. They answered,
"We're merchants; our boat is bringing
Food to market. We're selling   2540
Bread and wine, bacon
And ham, pork and beef,
And whoever wants it can buy it."
"Now praise the Lord," said
The defenders, "for making the wind   2545
Blow you here to our shore!
Welcome, welcome, good friends!
Disembark: you've sold
Everything at whatever price
You may ask. Just come and collect   2550
Your money: you won't be able
To count the gold and silver
We're going to give you for all
Your wheat, and your wine, and your meat.
Oh, we'll give you a cart   2555
To carry it off with, if you like,
Or more than one. We don't care!"
Thus buyers and sellers both
Concluded a good piece of business.
They hurried to unload the barge   2560
And carry in goods that would mean
So much to the castle's defenders.
        And when those inside saw
It was food they were bringing in,

You can ask yourself how happy   2565
They were, and how quickly they got
To work cooking and baking!
Now Clamadeu could wait
Outside as long as he wanted,
For those inside had plenty   2570
Of beef and pork and bacon,
And bread and wine and venison.
The cooks didn't waste a minute:
Boys put a match to the fires
And the cooks prepared the food.   2575
And the young lord of the castle
Could enjoy the girl at his leisure,
Her arms around him, kissing
And taking delight in each other.
The castle hall was quiet   2580
No longer, but once again noisy
With joy. All of them ate
As much as they wanted—and those
Who'd hurried to cook the food
Came to the table, too,   2585
As starved as everyone else.
They finally rose from their meal—
But Clamadeu and all
His men were already dying
Inside, having heard the news,   2590
Declaring they were ready to give up
The siege, for now the defenders
Couldn't be starved. They'd have
To leave; they'd been wasting their time.
Wild with rage, telling   2595
No one what he'd done, Clamadeu

Sent a messenger to the castle,
Informing the knight in red
That until the next day at noon
He could fight a battle, man   2600
To man in the open field,
If he dared. Hearing this message
Announced to her lover, the girl
Was worried and angry, but he replied
At once that, having asked   2605
For a fight, Clamadeu
Would have a fight, whatever
Might happen. The girl was twice
As unhappy, hearing this,
But no matter how sad he made her   2610
The young man meant to fight.
Men and women alike
Begged him not to accept
A challenge from Clamadeu,
Who'd never in his life been defeated.   2615
"Gentlemen," he said, "you'd do
Better to save your breath,
For no one in all the world
Could make me go back on my word."
No one dared continue   2620
Once he'd cut them off
Like this, so they took to their beds
And slept till dawn the next day,
But terribly sad that their lord
Could not be dissuaded, for all   2625
Their prayers, from this foolhardy combat.
That night the girl kept begging
Her lover not to fight

The battle, but stay home in peace,
For now they need no longer   2630
Fear either Clamadeu
Or his men. But nothing could move him—
A fact exceedingly strange,
Considering how well she blended
Caresses with sorrow, weeping   2635
At every word, kissing
So sweetly, so softly, that indeed
She turned the key of love
This way and that in his heart,
Yet never succeeded, whatever   2640
She did, in making him give up
The battle he'd pledged himself
To fight. He ordered his arms
And armor brought, and those
Who served him hurried to obey.   2645
But as they made him ready
They worked in sorrow, and wept,
Praying to the King of kings.
Then he mounted the Norwegian horse
He'd had them bring in, and rode off   2650
So quickly that he left them alone
With their tears and their sorrow, standing
Where he and his horse had been.
        When Clamadeu saw him coming,
And knew he meant to fight,   2655
He was sure the boy must be crazy;
He expected to quickly and easily
Sweep the boy from his saddle.
The field was flat and smooth,
And they were completely alone,   2660

For Clamadeu had sent
His men away, and they'd gone.
Both had their lances ready,
Resting on the saddle bow,
And they charged without a word   2665
Or the slightest delay. Both
Their spears were ashwood, with iron
Points; both were heavy
And sharp; both knights were strong
And spurred their horses, hating   2670
Each other, intending death.
The shock as they crashed together
Cracked both their shields,
Broke both their lances,
And threw both knights to the ground.   2675
But they jumped right up and immediately
Drew their glittering swords,
And began to slash at each other.
They fought on equal terms
And I could describe it all,   2680
If I wanted to take the time,
But it isn't worth the effort:
One word is as good as twenty.
Finally, Clamadeu
Was forced to surrender, in spite   2685
Of himself, and accept the boy's
Terms, as his steward had done,
For he had no more desire
For the dungeons of Beaurepaire
Than his steward had felt, and not   2690
For the vast empire of Rome
Would he let himself be imprisoned

By Gornemant of Goort.
So he gladly swore to ride
To King Arthur's court and become   2695
That king's captive and give
The boy's message to the girl
Kay had handled so roughly
(And to whom he'd given such pain):
If God gave him the strength   2700
The boy would surely avenge her.
And Clamadeu promised, too,
That before the dawn of another
Day he'd free all
The prisoners locked in his towers,   2705
And would never again so long
As he lived allow anyone
To attack the castle, but swore
To protect it, and neither he
Nor anyone would bother the girl.   2710
        So Clamadeu rode off
Homeward, and as soon as he got there
Ordered all his prisoners
Unconditionally freed,
Released without restrictions.   2715
This was the pledge he had made,
And this was what was done.
So out they came from his dungeons,
Carrying all their belongings,
Set free at the snap of a finger,   2720
Nothing and no one held back.
And Clamadeu himself
Set off on his lonely road.
In those days (these rules can be read

In books) the custom required 2725
A conquered knight to proceed
Into prison straight from combat,
Dressed exactly as he was,
Removing not a single
Garment nor adding one 2730
To what he was wearing. Armored,
And bearing his weapons, Clamadeu
Followed Anguinguerron,
His steward, to Disnadaron,
Where Arthur was holding court. 2735
Meanwhile, back in the castle,
They celebrated the captives'
Return, set free at last
After long suffering in miserable
Cells. And every lodging 2740
That held a knight rang
With joy. The bells of every
Church and monastery
Sounded, and monks and nuns
Gave grateful thanks to Our Lord. 2745
People were dancing up
And down the streets, and everywhere.
But those in the castle sang
Loudest, now safe from attack.
Meanwhile, Anguinguerron 2750
Rode toward the court, and his lord
Behind him, spending three nights
In a row where his steward had lodged.
Tracking his horse's hoofmarks,
Master followed man 2755
Straight to Disnadaron,

Where Arthur's court was in session.
So Clamadeu arrived,
Traveling alone and just
As he was, and his steward—already   2760
Delivered of the message he was bearing,
Spoken aloud in everyone's
Presence the day he'd come there—
Recognized his master.
The court had claimed the steward   2765
For itself. But despite his master's
Blood-spattered armor, the steward
Knew him, and immediately called out,
"Gentlemen, gentlemen, what a wonderful
Sight! By God, the boy   2770
In red armor must have sent you
The knight who's coming over there.
He beat him in battle, I'm sure of it,
Seeing the blood all over him.
I see the blood from here,   2775
And I'd know him anywhere,
For he is my lord, I'm his man.
His name is Clamadeu
Of the Islands, and there's no better
Knight in the Roman Empire.   2780
But even the best knights can fall."
These were Anguinguerron's words
As Clamadeu arrived,
And then they ran to each other,
Meeting in the middle of the court.   2785
        It was Pentecost. The queen
Was seated at King Arthur's side
As he sat at the head of the table.

Below him sat counts and kings,
Countesses and queens, 2790
Come to court after Mass,
Stately ladies and their knights
Leaving church together.
Sir Kay threw off his mantle
And crossed the great hall, his right hand 2795
Holding a small wand,
A felt hat on his head,
His long blond hair hanging
Down his back. No knight
In all the world could match 2800
His beauty—but his cruel, malicious
Tongue tarnished and blemished
His looks and his courage alike.
His tunic was made of rich
Multicolored silk; 2805
Around it he wore a handsome
Belt, its buckle and clasps
Of hammered gold (as I read
In the book where his costume is described).
Knights stepped out of his way 2810
As he walked through the hall, everyone
Fearing his savage taunts,
His savage tongue; they scurried
To safety, out of his path—
As well they might, for whether 2815
In jest or deadly serious
His words would fly like arrows.
No one there in that hall
Could help cringing away,
Silent, as he came stalking 2820

Straight to the king, and said,
"My lord, if you please, I could have
Dinner served right now."
"Kay," said the king, "leave me
In peace! By the eyes in my head,   2825
I refuse to eat, at a solemn
Feast like this, until
My court hears news of some wonder."
      Even as he spoke these words
Clamadeu came to his court,   2830
A vanquished knight, and a captive,
Appearing, as he had to, in full armor,
And said, "God's blessings on
The very best king in the world,
The bravest and noblest of all,   2835
According to those who've been
To his court and seen and heard of
His grand and glorious deeds!
And now please listen, your majesty,
As I give you the message I've brought.   2840
It pains me to admit, in open
Court, that I come here the captive
Of a knight who beat me in battle.
I've been ordered to surrender myself
To you; I have no choice.   2845
But if anyone here intends
To ask me if I know his name,
I must answer no, I don't.
All I'm able to say
Is that his armor is red   2850
And he told me he got it from you."
"My friend," said the king, "in the name

Of Our Lord, tell me the truth:
What state is he in? Is he healthy
In body and mind? Is he free?"   2855
"My lord," said Clamadeu,
"Rest assured: he is—
And surely the bravest knight
I've ever met in my life.
And he's told me to tell the girl   2860
Who laughed at Sir Kay, and whom
Sir Kay so shamed, slapping
Her face, that the blow would be
Avenged, if only Our Lord
In Heaven allowed it." Hearing   2865
These words, the king's fool
Jumped for joy, and cried,
"As God is my witness, my lord,
That blow will be well revenged.
This is no joke, for Kay   2870
Deserves a broken arm,
Or maybe a broken neck!
And he's going to get it!" Hearing
This charming prattle, Kay
Barely kept himself   2875
From cracking the fool's skull—
Not out of fear, but because
Of the king and the scandal it would cause.
    The king shook his head,
Saying, "Ah Kay, how sorry   2880
I am that he's not at my court!
Your wild tongue drove him
Away, and I deeply regret it."
Then, at the king's command,

Girflet rose to his feet,   2885
And my lord Yvain, whose company
Improved anyone he was with,
And following the king's instructions
These two noble knights
Led Clamadeu to the rooms   2890
Where the queen's ladies were busy
Amusing themselves. As the king
Had ordered, they brought him directly
To the girl Kay had slapped
In the face, and he gave her a message   2895
She was more than happy to hear,
For she still felt, in her heart
And on her cheek, the shame
And the pain of that blow. Her face
Had long since been cured of the purely   2900
Physical pain, but the blow
To her honor was not so easily
Cured, for she could not forget
The shame or forgive the man
Who'd caused her to feel it. No worthy   2905
Heart, beating strong
And hard, forgets such sorrow,
Though cowards let it grow cold.
Clamadeu delivered his message;
Then the king told him he'd remain   2910
At court the rest of his life.
But he who'd fought that knight —
Snatching Blanchefleur,
His beautiful belovèd, and her lands
From Clamadeu's grip — he lived   2915
In delight, and would have had her

And her lands forever, except
That his heart pulled him away,
Tugging in a different direction:
He remembered his mother, and the sight of her   2920
Fainting and falling to the ground,
And more than anything else
In the world he longed to see her
Again. His belovèd would not
Let him go; he dared not   2925
Ask her. She'd ordered all
Her people to beg him to stay—
But they begged in vain. Still,
He swore a solemn oath
That if he found his mother   2930
Alive, he'd bring her back
With him, then stay and defend
Those lands forever, as he also
Would, should his mother be dead.
        And so he set off, promising   2935
To return, leaving his lovely
Blanchefleur (and everyone
Else) both very angry
And also very sad.
And as he rode away   2940
The procession that followed behind him
Was like the feast of Ascension!*
All the monks were there,
Wearing silken cloaks
As if it had been a Sunday,   2945
And all the nuns with their veils,

* Commemorating Christ's ascension to Heaven

And everyone crying out,
"Lord, you led us out
Of exile and back to our homes:
Is it any wonder that we weep,   2950
Finding ourselves so soon
Abandoned? Our sorrow is so
Immense it's beyond human
Conception!" He answered, "There's nothing
To fear, believe me: nothing.   2955
Don't you think it right
And proper that I visit my mother,
Who lives alone in that vast
Wood, the Barren Forest?
I have to see her, living   2960
Or dead. I can't abandon her.
If I find her alive, I'll have her
Take the veil in your convent.
And if she's dead, you'll say
A yearly Mass for her soul,   2965
Which God will hold, with the other
Saints, in Abraham's bosom.
And you, monks and nuns:
Don't trouble yourselves, for I'll give you
Gifts in her name, if God   2970
Decides to return me here."
Then monks and nuns and all
The others left him. And he rode
On his way, lance at the ready,
Armed as he was when he came.   2975
He rode all day, meeting
No earthly soul, neither
Man nor woman who could help him

Find his way. Nor
Did he ever stop praying   2980
To the King of Glory, Our Father
In Heaven, to let him, should it be
His will, to see his mother
Again, alive and healthy.
Repeating this prayer, over   2985
And over, he came riding down
A slope and arrived at a river.
The water was deep and ran
So fast that he couldn't cross,
And he said, "Oh, Almighty God,   2990
If only I could cross this water
I know I'd find my mother
Alive and well!" He rode
Along the stream till he came
To a rocky cliff directly   2995
At the water's edge and could go
No farther. And then he saw
A craft descending the river,
With two men on board.
He paused, waiting for the boat   3000
To draw nearer, expecting
The current would surely carry them
Close to the bank. But instead
They stopped dead in the middle
Of the stream, completely motionless,   3005
Firmly anchored in place.
And then the man sitting
In the bow cast his line,
Baited with a fish as small
As a minnow. Not knowing what   3010

He could do to cross the river,
The boy called out, asking,
"Gentlemen, tell me, if you please,
Is there a bridge across
This river?" The man who sat there   3015
Fishing answered, "No,
My friend, by God! Nor
Will you find, I think, for twenty
Leagues in any direction,
A boat bigger than this one,   3020
Which carries no more than five men
And couldn't carry your horse —
No boat, no bridge, no ford."
"Then tell me," he said, "in the name
Of God, where I might   3025
Be able to find lodgings."
"That's just what you'll need, I think,
And other things, too. I'll be
Your host for the night: follow
The crack you'll see, right   3030
In that rock over there, ride up,
And when you get to the top
You'll see, in a valley in front of you,
The house I live in, with rivers
And forests all around it."   3035
He rode right up the crack
And got to the top. But as
He looked around him, all
He could see, in every direction,
Was the earth and the sky above it.   3040
"What am I hunting, up here?
Such a stupid waste of time!

May God heap infinite shame
On the man who sent me here!
He told me that when I reached   3045
The top of this cliff I'd see
The house he lived in! Fisherman,
Every word you said
Was a lie, and you said them all
To make me miserable." And then,   3050
In a valley far below,
He saw the top of a tower.
From there to Beirut there was nothing
Lovelier or better built.
It was crafted of gray-brown stone   3055
And ringed around with turrets.
The tower was in back of the living
Quarters, through which one entered.
The boy rode quickly down,
Swearing, now, that the man   3060
Who'd sent him had guided him well.
He was full of praise for the fisherman,
No longer calling him cheater
And trickster, disloyal, a liar,
Since he'd found his lodgings.   3065
He rode right up to the gate
And found a drawbridge, conveniently
Lowered for his use. He crossed
The bridge, and four servants
Came running out to greet him;   3070
Two helped him out of his armor,
The third led his horse to the stable,
To feed him hay and oats,
And the fourth draped on his shoulders

A fresh, clean scarlet cloak,   3075
And led him as far as the door.
Believe me, from there to Limoges
You could scour the land and not find
Anything so beautifully built.
And then he waited, in the entry   3080
Hall, to meet the lord
Of the castle. Two young servants
Appeared and led him into
The great hall, which was square,
Equal in length and breadth.   3085
Seated on a bed, in the middle
Of the hall, he saw a handsome
Knight with grizzled hair,
His head covered by a hat
As dark as a blackberry, wrapped   3090
Like a turban in purple cloth.
And all his clothing was black.
He lay leaning on his elbow,
And a blazing fire burned
Beside him, dry wood set   3095
In the center of four columns
With room for four times a hundred
Men to be seated around it,
Comfortably all at their ease.
These huge columns, straight   3100
And strong, supported a towering
Chimney, bronze and massive.
The servants conducting the guest—
One to the left, one
To the right—led him to his host,   3105
Who seeing them come immediately

Greeted the boy, saying,
"My friend, don't be offended
If I don't rise to give you
Welcome, because I can't." 3110
"Don't speak of it, Sir, in the name
Of Our Lord. I'm not bothered,
God having granted me joy
And health." With a great effort
The knight sat up as far 3115
As he could: "Come closer, my friend:
Don't be afraid. Come sit
Quietly at my side. It would make me
Exceedingly happy." So the boy
Went and sat beside him, 3120
And the knight inquired, "My friend,
Where have you come from today?"
"Sir," was the answer, "this morning
I started from Beaurepaire castle."
"My Lord!" said the knight. "How long 3125
A journey you've had. Surely,
You must have left before
The watchman sounded his morning
Horn." "Oh no," said the boy.
"I assure you: the day's first hour 3130
Had been signaled." As they spoke
A servant entered the hall.
A sword hung in a swordbelt
Slung from his shoulder, and he carried it
Straight to the lord of the castle, 3135
Who drew it partway from its sheath,
Looking at the words written
On the blade, which told where the weapon

Had been forged, and simultaneously
Seeing what splendid steel   3140
It was made of, impossible to break
Except in a single instance
Known only to the man
Who had done the hammering and forging.
And the servant who'd carried it in   3145
Said, "That golden-haired girl,
Your beautiful niece, has sent you
This sword as a gift. No weapon
So massive, so long, has ever
Been made so perfectly balanced.   3150
Decide for yourself who should have it,
But my lady will be wonderfully pleased
To have it used, and used well,
By whatever hand will wield it,
For the maker of this sword has forged   3155
Three and only three,
And having made this one
He will never make another."
Then the lord of the castle gave
Both sword and swordbelt (itself   3160
Easily worth a fortune)
To the stranger, his guest. The sword's
Rounded pommel was fine
Greek or Arabian gold;
The scabbard bore Venetian   3165
Embroidery. Having given his guest
So rich a gift, the host
Declared, "My friend, this sword
Was meant for you, and you
Alone, and I want you to have it.   3170

Buckle it on, and try it."
The boy thanked him, and buckled it
On, but not too tightly,
Then drew the naked blade
And having held the sword   3175
For a moment, put it back
In its scabbard. Believe me, it looked
Splendid at his side, and still better
In his hand: truly, he seemed
Someone who would use it well,   3180
When he had to. In the clear light
Of the fire, he could see, behind him,
The page in charge of his weapons
And armor, and handed him
The sword, to hold with the rest.   3185
And then he rejoined his host,
Who'd done him so great an honor.
They sat in a hall lit
As brightly as candles can make
An indoor room. And as   3190
They chatted of this and that,
A servant entered the hall,
Carrying—his hand at its center—
A white lance. He came out
Of a room, then walked between   3195
The fire and those seated
On the bed, and everyone saw
The white wood, and the white
Spearhead, and the drop of blood
That rolled slowly down   3200
From the iron point until
It reached the servant's hand.

The boy saw that wondrous
Sight, the night he arrived there,
But kept himself from asking   3205
What it might mean, for he'd never
Forgotten—as his master at arms
Had warned him, over and over—
He was not to talk too much.
To question his host or his servants   3210
Might well be vulgar or rude,
And so he held his tongue.
      And then two other servants
Entered, carrying golden
Candleholders worked   3215
With enamel. They were wonderfully handsome
Boys, and the candleholders
They each clasped in their hands
Bore at least ten
Burning candles. A girl   3220
Entered with them, holding
A grail-dish* in both her hands—
A beautiful girl, elegant,
Extremely well dressed. And as
She walked into the hall,   3225
Holding this grail, it glowed
With so great a light that the candles
Suddenly seemed to grow dim,

* The Old French word is *graal,* meaning cup, chalice, grail, and so
on. But as Poirion says, "Dans cette phrase, un graal (avec l'article
indéfini) est un objet en apparence quelconque" (In this sentence, a
grail [used with the indefinite article] is apparently an ordinary object
[p. 1349n])—that is, not *the* grail.

Like the moon and stars when the sun
Appears in the sky. Then another   3230
Girl followed the first one,
Bearing a silver platter.
The grail that led the procession
Was made of the purest gold,
Studded with jewels of every   3235
Kind, the richest and most costly
Found on land or sea.
No one could doubt that here
Were the loveliest jewels on earth.
Just as they'd done before,   3240
When carrying the lance, the servants
Passed in front of the knight,
Then went to another room.
And the boy watched them, not daring
To ask why or to whom   3245
This grail was meant to be served,
For his heart was always aware
Of his wise old master's warnings.
But I fear his silence may hurt him,
For I've often heard it said   3250
That talking too little can do
As much damage as talking too much.
Yet, for better or worse,
He never said a word.
The lord of the castle ordered   3255
Water brought and tablecloths
Spread, and those whose work
This was did what had
To be done. Then host and guest
Washed their hands in mildly   3260

Warmed water, and two servants
Brought in a large ivory tabletop
(The book where one reads this story
Says it was all of one piece).
They held it there a moment,   3265
As the two noblemen watched,
While two other servants
Brought in wooden supports
(Fashioned, we're told, of timber
Made totally indestructible   3270
For two remarkable reasons:
They'd been carved of ebony, and this wood
Never decays or burns,
So neither possible danger
Could ever occur). Then they set   3275
The ivory top over
The supports, and spread out the tablecloths.
What can I say of these cloths?
Ambassadors—cardinals—popes:
None could command such whiteness.   3280
Their first course was a haunch
Of rich venison, in pepper
Sauce; they drank their clear
Wine from golden cups.
The roasted meat was sliced   3285
Right in front of the diners
(The whole haunch having
Been carved on that silver platter),
And served, to host and guest,
On well-baked breadlike shells.   3290
Meanwhile, the wonderful grail
Was carried back and forth,

But again the boy was silent,
Not asking to whom it was served.
And again it was thoughts of his master   3295
Which kept him from speaking, for he never
Forgot how clearly he'd been warned
To beware of too much talking.
And so he stayed silent too long.
With every course, the grail   3300
Was borne back and forth,
Uncovered, plainly visible,
And still he did not know why.
Although he wished to know
He told himself he'd surely   3305
Make some safe inquiry
Before he left; someone
Would tell him. He'd wait until morning,
When he was taking leave of the lord
Of this castle and all who served him.   3310
And so he postponed his questions,
And simply ate and drank.
There was no shortage of food
Or wine, not at that table;
He dined in delight, and enjoyed it.   3315
       They ate exceedingly well:
The lord of the castle served
What kings and counts and emperors
Are supposed to eat, and the boy
Sat at the table beside him.   3320
And then, when dinner was done,
They spent the rest of the evening
Talking. Then servants prepared
Their beds and brought in exotic

Fruit for their final repast—   3325
Figs and dates, nutmeg,
Cloves, pomegranates,
And finally a healthy honey
Paste of Alexandrian
Ginger and other digestive   3330
Herbs that help the stomach
And soothe and calm the nerves.
They drank assorted fine
Liqueurs, neither sharp nor sweetened,
And well-aged wine, and clear   3335
Syrup. The boy was astonished;
He'd never heard of such things.
Then his host said, "My friend,
It's time we went to bed
For the night. If you've no objections,   3340
I'll sleep in my own room,
And whenever you wish to, you can sleep
Here. I cannot walk,
So they'll have to carry me out."
Then four strong and lively   3345
Men came into the hall;
Each one grasped a corner
Of the bed the lord lay on,
And picking him up, carried him
There where he needed to be.   3350
Other servants stayed
With the boy, to attend to his wants,
And gave him whatever he needed,
And when he wished to sleep
They took off his shoes and his clothes   3355
And laid him in the finest linens

And blankets. And he slept until morning—
Indeed, till the sun was well up
And the servants were bustling about.
But looking around, he saw   3360
None were in the room
Near him, so he had to rise
Unassisted. This was annoying,
But he saw it had to be done
And did it, alone, as best   3365
He could, shoes and all,
Then went to fetch his armor,
Which someone had brought and left
On top of a table. Once
His clothing and equipment were in place,   3370
He tried the doors to other
Rooms, all open the night
Before, but wasted his time,
For now they were locked. He banged
And called as loud as he could,   3375
But nothing was opened and no one
Responded. Tired of shouting,
He went to the hall's main door
And, finding it open, descended
The stairs. Coming to the bottom,   3380
He found his horse, all saddled,
And saw his lance and his sword
Leaning against a wall.
Mounting, he looked in every
Direction, and still saw no one: 3385
No soldiers, no pages, no serving
Men. Glancing to his right,
Toward the gate, he saw the drawbridge

Had been lowered and left unguarded;
He could enter, and he   3390
Could leave, whenever he liked,
Needing no permission.
The household servants, he thought,
Had probably gone to the woods,
Checking snares and traps,   3395
And left the drawbridge down.
He wanted to waste no more time,
But thought he might just ride
Behind them a bit, to ask,
If he could, why the lance   3400
Dripped blood (was some sorrow involved?)
And why they'd borne the grail.
He rode right out the gate.
But just as he got to the end
Of the drawbridge, he felt his horse's   3405
Hind feet rise in the air,
And the horse make a swift leap—
And had the animal jumped
Less well, they both might have been
Hurt, horse and rider   3410
Alike. Turning around,
Anxious to see what had happened,
He saw the drawbridge had been raised.
He called, but no one answered:
"You! You who raised   3415
The bridge, come out here! Talk to me!
How come I can't see you?
Step forward, let me see you!
There's something I want to ask you,
Something I want to know."   3420

He spoke like a fool: no one
Answered, and no one would—
So he rode into the forest,
Following a path that showed
Signs of fresh hoofmarks,   3425
A horse that had gone before him.
"That," he said to himself,
"Must be the fellows I'm hunting."
He rode on through the wood,
Following the trail, and suddenly   3430
Came upon a girl
Sitting under an oak tree,
Weeping and sighing as if
Afflicted with the worst sorrow
In the world. "Oh miserable one!"   3435
She cried. "Some evil star
Cursed the hour of my birth,
Bringing me into existence
To suffer every sort
Of pain, and escaping none!   3440
I wouldn't have lived to see
My belovèd dead, had God
So willed; He should have decreed
That Death, who brought me such sorrow,
Left him alive and killed me.   3445
Why leave me without my belovèd?
What is life worth, when all
I love best is dead? With him
Gone, both my life
And my body mean nothing to me.   3450
Take my soul, oh Death,
So I can go with him, and serve him,

If he'll stoop so low as to have me."
   And so she grieved, mourning
A knight who lay in her arms   3455
Dead, his head cut off.
Seeing and hearing her, the boy
Rode directly up
And stopped; he greeted the girl;
She bent her head, and returned   3460
His greeting, but went on weeping.
And he asked her, "Tell me,
Young lady, who killed that knight
Lying dead in your lap?"
"My lord," she said, "a knight   3465
Killed him, just this morning.
But one thing I see, as you stand there,
Seems to me astonishing:
A knight could ride, so help me
God (and as everyone knows),   3470
For twenty-five leagues, straight
Along the road you've come,
And never find decent
Lodging, clean and safe,
And yet your horse has been groomed   3475
And brushed, washed and combed,
His coat is clean and polished,
And he's clearly been given oats
And hay, for his belly is full—
And how his mane shines! You   3480
Yourself would seem to have spent
A restful, comfortable night
On some soft, well-made bed."
"Indeed I have, pretty lady,

In lodgings as good as one gets: 3485
I ought to seem well-rested!
But if anyone, standing right here,
Were to call in a loud, clear voice,
They'd hear him perfectly well
There where I slept last night.   3490
Plainly, you don't know this country
Well; you haven't explored it.
Oh, I had lodgings, all right!
The best I've ever had."
"My lord! Then were you lodged   3495
At the castle of the rich Fisher King?"
"By Christ, girl, I've no
Idea. But fisherman
Or king, he's courteous and wise.
I can't say any more,   3500
Though I met two men, last night,
Sitting in a boat that came gliding
Slowly along. The man in
The back steered; the man
In the front sat there and fished,   3505
And he was the one who said
He'd give me lodgings in his house."
"My lord," said the girl, "he's a king;
I can tell you that for certain.
He was wounded in battle, and so badly   3510
Hurt, so maimed, that without
Help he can't even walk.
A spear struck him right
Between the legs, and the pain
Is still so great that riding   3515
A horse is impossible. And when

He needs to amuse himself
A bit, to rest and relax,
He has himself put in a boat
And sits in the bow, fishing,   3520
And that's why he's called the Fisher
King. Fishing is his only
Distraction: every other
Sport or amusement is too painful.
He can't hunt for deer   3525
Or ducks, but his men catch fowl
For him, and roam through the woods,
Killing deer with their arrows.
Which is why he enjoys living
So close to this very spot,   3530
For nowhere in all the world
Could he find a place that suits him
Better. So he's built a house
Worthy of a rich king."
"By God, girl," he said,   3535
"Every word you say
Is true! I was astonished,
Last night, when I stood in his presence.
I kept my distance, at first,
But he told me to come and sit   3540
Beside him, and asked me not
To be offended if he didn't
Rise to greet me, because
He couldn't, he was wounded and weak.
So I went and sat beside him."   3545
"He showed you great honor, indeed,
Seating you at his side.
Tell me: seated there,

Did you see the spear that bled
Without the presence of flesh   3550
Or veins?" "Did I see it?
Oh yes, by God, I did!"
"And did you ask why
It was bleeding?" "I said not a word."
"In the name of God, believe me,   3555
You made a mistake. That was wrong.
Did you see the grail, too?"
"Quite clearly." "By whom was it carried?"
"A girl." "Where did she come from?"
"From a room." "And where did she go?"   3560
"Into some other room."
"Did anyone walk in front of her?"
"Yes." "Who?" "Two servants,
That's all." "And what were they holding?"
"Well-lit candleholders."   3565
"And who came after the grail?"
"A girl." "And what was she holding?"
"A small silver platter."
"Did you ask any of these people
Where they were going with these things?"   3570
"Not a word escaped my lips."
"Oh Lord, that's even worse!
My friend: tell me your name."
And then, not knowing his name,
He somehow knew, and said   3575
He was Perceval from Wales,
Not knowing if he spoke the truth,
But he did, though he did not know it.
And hearing this the girl
Rose and faced him, and spoke   3580

As if in anger, "You've just
Changed your name, my friend."
"Really?" "You're Perceval
The Unhappy, the Miserable, the Unfortunate!
Ah, how unlucky you are,   3585
For had you asked those questions
You could have completely cured
The good king of all his wounds:
He would have become entirely
Whole, and ruled as he should.   3590
How much good you'd have done!
Believe me, miseries will come,
Instead, for you and for others.
You're being punished for the sin
You committed against your mother,   3595
Who died, sorrowing for you.
I know you better than you
Know me. You don't know who I am,
But for many years I lived
In your mother's house, with you,   3600
For I'm your first cousin
And you are mine. I regret it
All equally—the fact
That you never asked what
The grail was, and to whom   3605
It was being brought, and your mother's
Death, and also the death
Of this knight, for whom I felt
Such affection, and held in my heart,
For he always called me his dearest   3610
Love, treating me just
As a noble knight should."

"Ah cousin," said Perceval,
"If all you've said is the truth,
Tell me how you know it?" 3615
"I know it," the girl declared,
"Because I was there when it happened,
And I saw her buried!" "May God
In His awful goodness be moved
To show her soul His mercy! 3620
You've told a terrible tale.
But now that she's in her grave
Why should I go on seeking,
When she was what I sought?
All I wanted was to see her. 3625
I'll travel in a different direction.
I'd be pleased if you wish to journey
With me—for believe me, that knight,
Lying there dead, will never
Help you again. Death 3630
For the dead, life for the living.
Come with me, and we'll go
Together. Staying all
Alone with this corpse is foolish:
Let's follow the fellow who killed him 3635
And I promise you, here and now,
Either he'll bring me to my knees
Or I'll beat him into submission."
And the girl, still weeping, unable
To stem the sorrow in her heart, 3640
Replied, "My lord, nothing
Could make me go with you,
Or leave him, until
I see him properly buried.

Take my advice and ride 3645
On the paved road—that way—
For that's the direction he took,
The cruel, haughty knight
Who killed my sweet belovèd.
Not that I'm trying to talk you 3650
Into pursuing him: no,
By God, no matter how much
I loathe him. I hate him as much
As if it were me he'd killed!
But where did you get that sword, 3655
Hanging at your left side—
A weapon that's never drawn blood
And that no one has drawn in need?
I know exactly where
It was made, and just who made it! 3660
Be careful: never trust it—
As sure as I'm standing here
It will break into pieces, the moment
You draw it in battle." "Good cousin,
One of my host's nieces 3665
Sent it, yesterday, and he gave it
To me. It seemed a wonderful
Reward, until you spoke,
But now I don't know. Are these things
You're telling me true? And tell me, 3670
Also, if you happen to know,
Can its maker ever be found,
Should it need to be repaired?"
"Yes. But it won't be easy.
To get this sword re-made, 3675
Hammered whole once more,

A man must know the way
As far as the Firth of Forth.
And if you find it, only
Trebuchet* can fix it.   3680
Let no other smith attempt it.
He made it, and he can repair it,
But no one else can ever
Succeed. Be careful! Any
Other smith laying   3685
A hand on this sword will fail."
"I'd be very sorry indeed,"
Said he, "if it broke." And then
He left, and she remained,
Unable to leave the dead man   3690
For whom she grieved so profoundly.
         Perceval came upon
The track of an exhausted,
Staggering palfrey that had gone
The way he was going, and followed it.   3695
And soon he saw it, all skin
And bones, so wasted that it seemed
Clear to him it had fallen
Into savage hands, ridden
Hard and poorly fed,   3700
Like a borrowed horse one rides
The whole day long but never
Thinks about at night.
That's just how this palfrey looked —

* A smith with a reputation that must have rivaled that of the god Vul-
can. Poirion adds that "the reputation of weaponry is such that (not
only in the days of knighthood) a maker of fine swords is something
very like a magician" (p. 1353n).

So miserably thin that it trembled   3705
And shook as if it had palsy,
Its mane cut off, its ears
Hanging halfway to the ground.
Every dog that saw it
Slobbered, expecting a feast,   3710
For all that was left of the beast
Was the skin that covered its bones.
The woman's saddle on its back
And the harness on its head looked
As if they belonged where they were,   3715
And no one's seen a sorrier
Girl than the one who sat
In that saddle. Had she been living
Well, she could have been beautiful,
But life had treated her so badly   3720
That nowhere, on the dress she wore,
Could you find a palm-length of unripped
Fabric; her breasts protruded
Through the rips and tears in front.
Knotted thread and rough   3725
Stitching held her clothes together,
And her skin, having been beaten
And burned by snow and hail
And frost, was scratched and cracked
As if marked by some pointed tool.   3730
Her hair was all wild; she wore
No cloak. Her face bore the signs
Of endlessly streaming tears,
And so did her body: like waves
They'd come pouring down as far   3735
As her breasts, and then, under

Her dress, gone rolling all
The way to her knees. Whoever
Had known such fierce misery
Surely had a heart full of sorrow!   3740
As soon as Perceval saw her
He galloped over as fast
As he could, and she tried to hold
Her dress together and hide
Her flesh. But each tug   3745
That closed one gap opened
A hundred others instead.
      Her complexion discolored and pale,
She filled Perceval with pity.
As he came closer he heard   3750
The sad complaint of her misery
And pain: "Oh God," she cried,
"I beg you, please, don't let me
Live like this much longer!
This misery has lasted so long,   3755
And I don't deserve it! I've suffered
Far too much! Oh God,
You know—surely You know!—
None of this is deserved,
So send me, please, dear Lord,   3760
Someone who'll free me from this—
Or free me Yourself from the man
Who's forced me to such a life
Of shame. He shows me no mercy;
There's no way I can escape,   3765
And he has no desire to kill me,
Though why he wants me like this
I haven't the slightest idea,

Except that he finds my shame
And misery warm his heart. 3770
But even if the worst were true,
And I did deserve this treatment
At his hands, then having paid me
Back, he ought to be merciful,
If I've ever in any way pleased him. 3775
Certainly, he no longer loves me—
Not when he condemns me
To so harsh a love and remains
Indifferent." Perceval cried,
"Beauty, God has saved you!" 3780
Hearing these word, she lowered
Her head and replied, softly,
"My lord, you who've addressed me,
May you have your heart's desire,
Though it isn't right to say so." 3785
Embarrassed, Perceval blushed,
Then said to her: "Ah,
Young lady: why not? I don't
Believe I've ever seen you
Before, or done you wrong— 3790
Indeed, I'm sure." "Yes,
You have," she said, "but I've fallen
So low and suffered so much
That no one knows me any more.
If anyone greets me, or even 3795
Sees me, I sweat with fear."
"Indeed," he said, "whatever
I've done I've quite forgotten.
I'd no intention of causing
You pain. In fact, I came 3800

This way entirely by accident.
And the moment I saw you
So miserably poor, so naked,
May my heart enjoy no pleasure
If I thought of anything except   3805
What might have happened to bring you
To such a sorrowful state."
"My lord," she said, "have mercy!
Just be quiet and go
Away; leave me in peace.   3810
You were wrong to stop as you have—
But believe me, you need to leave!"
"Why should I flee?" he asked.
"Tell me. As far as I know
No one's pursued me here."   3815
"My lord," she said, "don't
Be angry: just flee while you can.
Don't let the Haughty Knight
Find you here with me.
There's nothing he likes better   3820
Than fighting and combat, and if
He finds you talking to me
He'll surely kill you on the spot.
It makes him so angry if anyone
Stops and spends a moment   3825
With me, that whoever he comes on
Has his head cut off.
Another knight just lost
His life. But before he kills them,
He tells them why he's forced me   3830
To lead a life like this."
While they were talking, the Haughty

Knight himself emerged
From the wood and galloped over
The dusty field like lightning,   3835
Crying, "You! You've done it
Now, talking to her!
You can't get away, I've got you!
Your life is over, I'll kill you
Here and now! But first,   3840
Before I cut off your head,
I'll tell you exactly why
This girl lives in such shame,
And what she's done. Now open
Your ears: here's the whole story.   3845
          "I went to the wood, one day,
And left this girl alone
And unattended in my tent,
She being my only
Love, when as it happened   3850
Some young Welshman came along.
How he did it I don't know,
But he managed to make her kiss him:
She told me so herself.
But she might have lied: perhaps,   3855
After that stolen kiss,
He decided to take the rest?
And who could believe he stopped
At a single kiss—for one thing
Leads to another. Anyone   3860
Who gets away with kissing
A girl, when they're all alone,
And stops right there, has got
To be stupid: a woman who's willing

To surrender her mouth will give   3865
Away the rest, if it's wanted.
And who doesn't know how women
Defend themselves? They always
Fight and win—except
In that one desperate battle   3870
Where she's got a man by the throat,
Scratching and biting to the death,
And all she wants is to lose.
She fights, but she gets impatient;
She can't just say she wants to,   3875
She wants him to make her yield,
So she won't feel guilty, or grateful.
That's why I think he took her—
Besides, he also stole
My ring, which she had on her finger.   3880
That made me very mad.
There's more: he drank a lot
Of my wine, and most of three venison
Pies I was saving for myself.
So now you can see how well   3885
I've paid my belovèd back!
Do wrong, and you pay: there's no other
Way to teach people lessons.
And now you can understand
My anger, seeing you with her.   3890
I'm angry, and I have a right!
And so I've said her palfrey
Will never eat again,
Or be cared for, or have new iron
Hooves, and she herself   3895
Will wear only what's on

Her back right now, until
I find the man who forced her,
And kill him, and cut off his head."
          Perceval listened to this,   3900
Then said, indifferent to his anger,
"My friend, she can surely stop
Her penitence, now, because
The man who kissed her against
Her will, and made her so sad,   3905
Was me. And I took her ring,
But that was all I took.
And yes, I admit I ate
One of your pies and half
Of another, and I drank your wine: 3910
Should a hungry man abstain?"
"By my head!" said the Haughty Knight.
"What a marvelous answer you've made me,
Admitting all these things!
And now you deserve to die,   3915
Confessing your sins as you have."
"Perhaps my death is not
So close," said Perceval.
Without another word
They galloped their horses, smashing   3920
Together with such force that both
Lances were shattered to bits
And both knights were hurled
From the saddle and thrown to the ground.
Quickly, they jumped to their feet,   3925
Drew their swords and began
Delivering mighty blows.
          They fought fiercely, and hard.

But why tell it all?
I've no interest in wasting   3930
My time. They fought till the Haughty
Knight admitted defeat
And was forced to beg for mercy,
And the boy, who never forgot
His master's warning not   3935
To deny mercy to any
Knight who begged to be spared,
Said, "Knight, by God,
I'll have exactly as much
Mercy on you as you show   3940
To your lady, who never deserved—
And I can swear it!—the terrible
Things you've made her endure."
          And the knight, who loved her more
Than his eyes, said, "Sir, I'll make   3945
Whatever amends you demand.
There's nothing you can ask
That I'm not prepared to do.
My heart aches for the painful,
Black-hearted things I've done."   3950
"Then go to the nearest house
You own, here in this region,
And let her bathe and rest
Until she recovers her health,
And when she's ready—looking   3955
As she should, dressed as she should—
Bring her to King Arthur, greet him,
And equipped exactly as you are
Place yourself in his hands.
If he asks who sent you to his court   3960

Tell him you come from the Knight
In Red—knighted by him
On his steward, my lord Kay's,
Advice. And tell the king,
In front of all the court,   3965
The pain and wicked suffering
You've caused this girl; make sure
That all of them hear you, as well
As the queen and all her ladies,
And the rest of the other lovely   3970
Women around her. But the one
I wish you to single out
Is she who laughed, seeing me,
And received, for that laugh, a stunning
Blow in the face from Sir Kay.   3975
You're to search her out
And tell her, at my command,
That the Knight in Red will never
Attend King Arthur's court
Until that blow is avenged—   3980
And that should make her happy."
The beaten knight declared
He'd gladly go, and say,
And do exactly as ordered,
Without delay, neglecting   3985
Nothing whatever, just
As soon as his love was properly
Taken care of. He'd also
Be very happy to lead
His conqueror home, and see him   3990
Rested and well, all
His wounds and bruises healed.

"Then go, and God go with you,"
Said Perceval. "But forget about me:
I'll seek another lodging."   3995
     Then all the talking was done,
And no one lingered any longer,
But left and went on their way.
That very night the girl
Was bathed, and beautifully dressed,   4000
And treated so wonderfully well
That all her beauty was restored.
And then, together, they rode
Directly to Carlion, where Arthur
Was holding, in private, a festive   4005
Court, in sign of which
The king was attended by only
Three thousand worthy knights.
Everyone saw the captive
Come, leading his lady   4010
Into King Arthur's presence
And declaring, when he stood before him,
"My lord, I stand here your prisoner,
Prepared to obey your commands
As I've been ordered to,   4015
In justice and right, by my conqueror,
The man who asked of you, and to whom
You gave, the armor of the Knight
In Red." These words were enough;
The king understood at once.   4020
"Remove your armor, good sir,"
He said. "May the knight who sent you
Live in pleasure and joy;
You yourself are welcome.

You will be treated well   4025
And honored, here in my house."
"My lord, there's more I must do.
Before I remove my armor
Let me ask this favor: may the queen
And the maids who attend her come   4030
And hear the news I bring
To you and to them, for my orders
Do not allow me to speak
Till the girl comes—she
Who was struck in the face for daring   4035
To laugh—just once, and only
For that, and nothing more."
And then he ceased to speak.
Hearing that the queen was needed,
The king called her to his presence,   4040
And she came, her maids with her,
Hand in hand, in pairs.
            And when the queen was seated
Near her lord the king,
The Haughty Knight spoke   4045
Once more: "My lady, I give you
Greetings from a noble knight
For whom I have great respect,
Who beat me in man-to-man combat—
Which is all I know of him,   4050
Except that he sends you my belovèd,
This girl, here at my side."
"My friend, I thank him warmly,"
Said the queen. And then he told them
All the villainy   4055
And shame he'd heaped on the girl,

And the suffering she'd had to endure.
He told them everything, including
His reasons, holding nothing
Back. And when they'd shown him   4060
The girl Kay had struck,
He said, "Girl, the knight
Who sent me here also
Sends you his greetings, commanding
Me to do nothing before   4065
I told you this: in the name
Of God, he'll never attend
Arthur's court, or assist
The king, until he's somehow
Able to revenge the blow   4070
You were given, the insult and the slap
You received on his account."
Hearing these words, the king's
Fool jumped up, crying,
"Sir Kay, as God is my judge,   4075
You're going to pay—oh yes!
And we won't be waiting too long."
          And then the king declared,
"Ah, Kay! How wrong you were
To mock the boy as you did.   4080
Your discourtesy drove him away,
And I fear he'll never return."
Then the king commanded the captive
Knight to take a seat
At court, released from all bonds,   4085
And he ordered his armor removed.
And then Sir Gawain, sitting
At the king's right hand, inquired,

"My lord, who could he be,
By God, able to defeat   4090
So noble a knight as this
In combat? Nowhere on all
The islands in the sea have I heard
Of such a knight, or known
Or seen one, performing the feats   4095
Of knighthood this boy has shown us!"
"Good nephew, neither have I,"
Said the king. "He came to my court,
But when I met him it never
Occurred to me to ask him   4100
Why, for he told me at once
He'd come to be made a knight.
And seeing so handsome a stranger,
I said: 'Gladly, my friend.
But dismount, if you will, and wait   4105
While I have them bring you golden
Armor.' He answered, no,
He wouldn't, and refused to dismount,
Saying all he wanted
From me was bright red armor.   4110
He said other strange things,
Explaining that the armor he wanted
Was worn, at the moment, by another
Knight, who had my golden
Cup. And Kay, who was being   4115
Nasty, as he always was
And is, and will be, speaking
No good, said, 'Brother, the king
Will let you have what you want.
Just go and get it for yourself.'   4120

And the boy, not seeing the joke,
Thought he was telling the truth,
And rode right out and killed
The knight in red armor with a dart.
I've no idea exactly 4125
How that fight started, but I know
The Red Knight, from the Forest
Of Quincroy, struck him—
But I don't know why—with his spear,
And made him angry, and he threw 4130
A dart right in the center
Of the eye, and killed him, and stripped off
His armor, and took it for himself.
And that was so very agreeable
To me that, by Saint David, 4135
To whom Welshmen pray,
I vow never to sleep
Indoors, two nights in a row,
Until I see him again,
On land or sea, if he lives. 4140
And now I'll go and find him!"
        Once the king had sworn
This oath, everyone knew
They had to pack up and leave.
You should have seen the linen 4145
Laid into trunks, and blankets,
And pillows, the horses loaded,
The wagons and carts filled up—
And no one could count the number
Of awnings and tents! Even 4150
A well-trained scribe, writing
From dawn to dusk, couldn't list

The harnesses and equipment
They prepared and carried with them.
The king left Carlion,   4155
Followed by all his barons,
As if he were off to war.
Nor did the girls stay at home,
For the queen swept them along,
To add to the honor and glory.   4160
That night, out in a field,
They slept alongside a wood,
And as they slept snow
Fell, and the country was cold;
Perceval had arisen early,   4165
As he always did, wanting
To hunt for adventure and the chance
To prove how brave he could be,
And riding across the fields,
Beneath the frigid sun,   4170
He came to the king's camp
But saw, before he reached
The tents, a flock of wild
Geese, dazzled by the heavy
Snow, fleeing as fast   4175
As birds can fly from a diving
Falcon dropping out of
The sky. It struck at a single
Goose, lagging behind
The others, and hit it so hard   4180
That it fell to the earth. But the hawk
Didn't follow it down, not hungry
Enough to take the trouble,
Too lazy to chase it. So the falcon

Flew off. But Perceval rode   4185
To where the goose had fallen.
The bird's neck had been wounded,
And three drops of blood
Had come rolling out on the snow,
Dying it vivid red.   4190
The bird had not been badly
Hurt, just knocked to the earth,
And before the knight could reach it
It had flown away in the sky.
But its body's oval shape   4195
Was printed in the snow, the blood-
Dyed color suffused inside it,
And Perceval, leaning on his lance,
Sat staring at the sight. Blood
And snow so mixed together   4200
Created a fresh color,
Just like his belovèd's face,
And as he stared he forgot
What he was doing and where
He was. The red stain   4205
Against the white snow
Seemed just like her complexion.
The more he looked, the happier
He grew, seeing once
Again the exact color   4210
Of her beautiful face. The morning
Slowly passed away,
And still he sat there musing,
Until at last squires
And pages emerged from the tents   4215
And saw him, and thought him asleep.

The king was still asleep,
Lying in his tent, but the wild
Knight named Sagremor
Was standing in front of the king's   4220
Tent, and he called to them:
"Tell me the truth," he said,
"And the whole truth, hiding
Nothing. Why are you out here
So early?" "My lord," they answered,   4225
"We've seen an unknown knight
Out there, sleeping on his horse."
"Armed?" "Oh yes, indeed!"
"I'll go and talk to him," he said,
"And then I'll bring him to court."   4230
But the first thing he did was enter
The king's tent, and wake him.
"My lord," he said, "there's a knight
Out there, sleeping on his horse."
And the king told him to speak   4235
To the knight, and ask him to join them
At court, not stay in the snow.
　　　　Sagremor ordered his horse
Brought out, and with it his weapons
And armor. The horse was led out   4240
And saddled, and they quickly buckled
On his armor. And fully prepared,
He rode away from the army,
And rode right up to the knight.
"Sir," he said, "you need   4245
To come to court." It was
As if he had not spoken.
So he said it again, and again

The knight did not move. And then
He grew angry: "By Saint Peter and Paul,   4250
Like it or not, you're coming!
I'm sorry I even bothered
To ask, for speaking to you
Is a waste of words!" And then
He unfurled the banner wound   4255
Round his lance, spurred his horse
The proper distance away,
Then wheeled and faced the knight
And charged, shouting, "Take care!
Take care!" to keep from attacking   4260
By surprise. Looking up,
Perceval saw him coming
And putting his thoughts aside
Galloped directly at him.
The shock of their smashing together   4265
Broke Sagremor's lance,
But Perceval's barely bent,
Striking so fierce a blow
That Sagremor fell from the saddle,
And his horse quickly turned   4270
And trotted briskly away
To the tents, its head held high.
Most of the king's barons
Saw this with little pleasure,
But Kay couldn't keep his nasty   4275
Tongue from wagging, and turning
To the king, he joked, "My lord,
Sagremor's coming back.
He's got that knight by the bridle
And now he'll bring him to court!"   4280

"Kay," said the king, "you're wrong
To mock at worthy knights.
Ride out yourself: let's see
If you can do any better."
"My lord," said Kay, "I'm delighted   4285
You'd like me to try. You
Can be sure I'll bring that fellow
Back, if he likes it or not,
And I'll make him tell you his name."
      Quickly, he got himself ready.   4290
And then, fully armed,
Rode toward the musing knight
Who was staring, lost in thought,
At the same three drops in the snow.
And Kay cried from far off,   4295
"You there! You there! Come
To the king! You'll either come
Right now, or pay for it dearly!"
Swinging his horse around,
He faced Perceval, then dug in   4300
His steel spurs and made
The animal gallop like the wind.
Both knights meant to win,
And they came together with a crash.
But Kay's blow, delivered   4305
With all his strength, broke
His lance into little pieces.
Not lacking in courage, Perceval
Aimed his lance straight
At the shield, and Kay was smashed   4310
Down on a rock; his collarbone
Dislocated, his left arm

Snapped, like a dry twig,
Between elbow and armpit, exactly
As the king's fool had predicted,   4315
Time and time again:
Prophetic words, and true ones!
Kay fainted from the pain.
Then his horse, too, turned
And trotted to the king's tents.   4320
And all the Britons watched
As the horse came home without
The steward. Pages rode out
To fetch him, and the whole court
Lamented. Seeing Kay   4325
So still, they thought he was dead.
The king was deeply affected;
Ladies and knights were in mourning.
But Perceval leaned on his lance
And stared at the three drops,   4330
Seeing his belovèd's face.
But Kay was only wounded.
Although the king was upset,
They told him not to worry,
For the steward could be cured—   4335
But they needed a surgeon who could put
The collarbone in place
And set the broken armbone.
So the king, whose affection for Kay
Was deep and lasting, sent for   4340
A wise, experienced surgeon,
Who came with three young female
Apprentices, who restored the collarbone
To its proper place, re-

Aligned and bound up the broken   4345
Bone, then brought Sir Kay
To the king's tent, explaining
That the fracture would heal well
And no one need be concerned.
And my lord Gawain declared,   4350
"Your majesty, as God is my witness,
It's wrong (as you know yourself,
For I've often heard you say so,
And you've given judgments accordingly)
For any knight to intrude on   4355
Another knight's thoughts, whatever
They may be, as these two have done.
Perhaps they were right, perhaps
They were wrong: I don't know. But one thing
Is sure: it didn't go well.   4360
The stranger knight might
Be thinking of someone he's lost;
His belovèd might have been stolen,
And his heart grieving and sad.
But if you like, I'll go   4365
And have a look, and should he
Be free of absorbing thoughts
I'll speak to him and ask
If he'd like to visit your court."
Hearing these words, Kay   4370
Grew angry: "My lord Gawain,
You'll go and lead him by the hand,
Saying nothing to displease him,
And that will be fine with him!
Of course he'll come—and you'll   4375
Still be king of the hill!

How many knights have you captured
Like that? Knights grow weary,
Fighting's too much like work—
And then you ask the king   4380
For permission to take them prisoner!
Damn me, Gawain! You're not
As stupid as you seem; there are things
To be learned from watching you.
You know how to talk, all right—   4385
Pretty, and polished, and polite.
Will you boast to this fellow, push him
With wicked, angry talk?
Whatever you say, whatever
He thinks, remember, I know   4390
Your game! Just wear a silken
Tunic: for this sort of battle
You'll never need to draw
A sword or break a lance.
Unless your tongue fails you,   4395
You're bound to win. Just tell him,
'Sir, may God protect you
And give you long life and good health,'
And he'll do whatever you like.
I can't pretend to teach you: 4400
Your tongue produces soft words
Like caresses on a cat. 'Oh Gawain's
Fighting hard,' they'll all
Be saying, watching you at work."
"Kay, my friend, you might   4405
Have spoken a bit more pleasantly.
You're angry—and you feel like venting
Your spite and spleen on me?

I'll bring him back, all right,
My good friend, if he can be brought,   4410
And I won't have a broken arm
Or a collarbone bent out of place:
No one treats me like that."
          "Nephew, go on," said the king.
"You've spoken as a good knight should.   4415
If he will come, bring him—
But go in your armor, weapons
In hand; you can't go disarmed."
And so that best of all knights
In merit and worth quickly   4420
Put on his armor, and mounted
A strong and agile horse,
And rode straight to where
The knight was leaning on his lance,
Still lost in delightful reflections   4425
On the face he fancied he saw
In the snow. But the sun, well up
In the sky, had melted away
Two of the three drops of blood;
The morning was well along,   4430
And Perceval's thoughts were not
So tightly gripped as before.
Gawain approached him, carefully
Letting his horse amble,
Showing no sign of hostility,   4435
Then said, "Sir, I'd give you
Greetings, if I knew the depths
Of your heart as I know my own.
But let me tell you, at least,
That I come as the king's messenger.   4440

He's sent me to say that he'd like
To have you attend his court."
"Two have already been here,"
Said Perceval, "trying to deprive me
Of my joy and pleasure, attempting   4445
To lead me away like a captive,
When all I wanted to do
Was relish these lovely thoughts.
And those who sought to take me
Away didn't care what was best   4450
For me, for here in the snow
Were three drops of fresh blood
Glittering against the snow.
And to me it seemed as if
I was seeing my beautiful belovèd's   4455
Fresh and shining face,
And my eyes wouldn't look away."
        "Indeed," said my lord Gawain,
"These are no vulgar thoughts,
But sweet and courteous both,   4460
And ripping them out of your heart
Would be foolish and brutally harsh.
Still, I should like to know,
If you please, what you mean to do
Now. If you wouldn't mind,   4465
I'd like to bring you to the king."
"Tell me, my good sweet friend,"
Said Perceval, "and tell me truly:
Is Kay the king's steward?"
"Yes, he is indeed,   4470
And let me tell you, too,
He was the second knight

You fought, and he paid for it dearly:
In case you don't know, you broke
His left arm and dislocated   4475
His collar-bone." "Then the girl
He struck has had her revenge,"
Said Perceval. And hearing
These words, my lord Gawain
Fairly leaped with surprise,   4480
And said, "Sir, by God
It's you the king has been hunting!
Please: tell me your name."
"Perceval, sir. And you?"
"Gawain." "Gawain?" "Indeed."   4485
Perceval's joy was immense.
"Good sir, I've heard you mightily
Praised, in many places,
And deeply desired that you
And I might be friends, unless   4490
The idea displeases you."
"Sir," said my lord Gawain,
"That pleases me no less
Than you, or even more!"
Then Perceval said, "By God,   4495
In that case I'll gladly go
With you—it seems only right.
Let me confess, I think
Better of myself for being
Your friend!" They rushed together   4500
And warmly embraced one another,
And each began to unlace
His helmet, and lower his visor,
And strip away the iron

Mail shirt he wore. And then   4505
They rode along together,
Happily, and the young servants
Who'd been watching all that happened
Went running in from their posts
And came straight to the king.   4510
"Lord, lord! By God,
Sir Gawain's coming, and leading
That knight, and they're showing each other
Great pleasure and rare delight."
All who heard this news   4515
Went running out of the tent
To greet the two who were coming.
And Kay said to the king,
"So now your nephew, my lord
Gawain, has earned high honor   4520
And praise. What a hard battle
He fought, in perfect safety,
For here he comes marching back
As blithe as when he went,
Having neither received   4525
Nor given a single blow,
Nor suffered the slightest damage.
'Oh how he deserves our praise!'
Everyone will say, succeeding
So well where those other fellows   4530
Failed—no matter how hard
We tried. Our efforts were useless."
And so spoke Kay, right
Or wrong, venting his feelings
As usual. But Gawain preferred   4535
Not to conduct his new friend

To court, wearing his armor.
So he took him to his tent and had him
Disarmed, and one of his servants
Brought proper clothing from a trunk   4540
And gave it to Perceval to wear.
      And when he was handsomely dressed
In a coat and cloak of perfect,
Resplendent fit, Gawain
Led him, hand in hand,   4545
To the king, waiting at the door
Of his tent. "My lord," said Gawain,
"I bring you, now, the knight
You've wanted so much to know,
These last two weeks, and he comes,   4550
As you see, of his own free will.
This is he of whom
You've spoken, and for whom you've longed.
Behold him, here he is!"
"Good nephew, I give you great thanks,"   4555
Said the king, rising at once
To greet his guest, declaring,
"Good sir, how welcome you are!
I beg you to tell me, please,
What name I should call you by."   4560
"By God, I'll hide nothing,
Your majesty, my lord:
I'm Perceval from Wales."
"Ah, Perceval, my friend!
Now that you've come to my court   4565
I hope you'll never leave!
I've deeply regretted, after
The first time we saw you here,

Not understanding the goodness
God holds in store for you.   4570
And yet it was clearly predicted
For my court and understood
By my fool and the girl Sir Kay,
My steward, struck in the face.
You've now fulfilled that prediction   4575
In every detail; there's not
The slightest doubt—and the latest
News confirms your worth."
   Just then the queen came in,
Having heard the news   4580
Of Perceval's arrival.
He saw her at once, and was told
Just who she was, and saw
Walking behind her the girl
Who had laughed at the sight of him;   4585
He went straight to the queen,
Saying, "May God grant joy
And honor to the best and loveliest
Lady in all the world—
For so say all who see her   4590
And all who ever have!"
And the queen said, in reply,
"And you are exceedingly welcome,
For you've proven yourself a knight
Of immense virtue and worth!"   4595
Then Perceval greeted the girl
Who had laughed when he first appeared
At court, and throwing his arms
Around her, gave her a hug
And said, "My beauty, if you need   4600

My service, remember, this
Is a knight who will never fail you."
And the girl thanked him as she should.
      The king and queen and all
The barons with them rejoiced   4605
At Perceval the Welshman's
Coming, and led him back
To Carlion that very same evening.
They celebrated all night,
And the next day, too, and then   4610
On the third day of his coming to court
A girl came riding up
On a tawny mule, her right hand
Holding a whip. She wore
Her hair in two black,   4615
Immense, and ugly braids,
And if the book that tells us
About her are truthfully written
No creature has ever seemed
So awful, not even at the bottom   4620
Of Hell. You'll never see
Iron as black as her neck
And hands, but her hands and neck
Were not her ugliest parts.
Her eyes were two deep caves,   4625
Smaller than the eyes on a rat,
And her nose was a monkey's, or a cat's,
With a donkey's ears—or a cow's.
Her teeth were as yellow as an egg,
But darker, more like rust,   4630
And she wore a beard, like a goat.
A hump grew in the middle

Of her chest, and her back was crooked,
And her thighs and shoulders were perfectly
Made for dancing—oh the hump   4635
On her back and her twisted legs
Were beautifully made for leading
A ball! Riding her mule,
She came right up to the king,
Who had never seen such a lady   4640
At a royal court. She greeted
The king and all his barons
As one—but Perceval
She addressed by name, speaking
From her perch on the tawny mule: 4645
"Ah Perceval, my friend,
Fortune is bald behind,
But hairy in front! May curses
Fall on whoever greets you
Or wishes you well or prays   4650
For your soul: you found Fortune
But didn't know how to keep it.
The Fisher King made you
His guest, you saw the bleeding
Lance, but you couldn't be bothered   4655
To open your mouth and speak,
Asking why that drop
Of blood came rolling down
From the point of that shining spear!
You saw the grail carried   4660
In, and never asked
For what great lord it was borne!
Those who see their chance
But never grasp it, hoping

For a better, must suffer for their failure.   4665
You're that unlucky man
Who watched opportunity
Arrive, and held his tongue.
What an unlucky fool!
How wrong to sit there, silent,   4670
When just a simple question
Could have cured that rich
And noble king of his suffering,
Allowed him to rule his kingdom
In peace. But now he never   4675
Will. Do you know what will happen,
Now that he'll never be cured,
Never be able to rule
His own lands? Ladies will lose
Their husbands, countries will be ruined,   4680
Girls will have no guidance
And be forced to linger as orphans,
And a host of knights will die,
And all because of you."
And then she turned to the king: 4685
"King, don't mind if I leave you.
I've a long, long way to go
Before I can sleep, tonight.
Tell me: have you ever heard
Of Castle Pride—for that's   4690
Where I need to go. That castle
Contains five hundred and sixty-
Six worthy knights,
And every single one
Keeps his belovèd at his side—   4695
Noble ladies, and lovely.

The only reason I tell you
Such things is this: no one
Goes to that castle expecting
Knightly combat and fails   4700
To find it. If they want it, they have it.
But he who wants the greatest
Honor in the world, I can tell him
Exactly where he can win it,
The precise region on earth—   4705
If he dares make the attempt.
Just down from the peak of Mount
Esclair a young lady's besieged:
Whoever can lift that siege
And free the girl will win   4710
The greatest honor to be won.
But not only fame: he'll also
Receive, and God will allow him
To wear without fear, the Sword
Hung from a Magic Sheath."   4715
    The young woman had finished speaking,
And having said what she wanted
To say, she turned and left.
Then Gawain jumped to his feet,
Declaring he'd do everything   4720
He could to rescue the girl,
And Girflet, Nudd's son,
Said with God's help he'd go
Straight to Castle Pride.
"And I'll climb Danger Mountain,"   4725
Said Kaerdin, "right to the top,
Without a single pause."
But Perceval disagreed,

Saying he'd never spend
Two nights in a row in any   4730
Lodging, or hear of any
Strange voyage and not test
Its strangeness, or learn of a worthy
Knight, or pair of knights,
Without offering to fight them—   4735
All this, until he knew
For whom the grail had been borne
And until he'd found the bloody
Lance and understood
Why it bled. These   4740
Were things he would do, whatever
It cost him. And fifty knights
Leaped up, vowing one
And all they'd follow every
Adventure, fight in every   4745
Battle, no matter where
On earth it took them. And as
They were making these declarations,
Who should they see entering
The hall but Guinganbresil,   4750
Carrying a golden shield
Painted with a blue band
So broad and thick that it easily
Covered a third of the span,
Measured in any direction.   4755
Guinganbresil knew and correctly
Greeted the king, but gave
No greeting to my lord Gawain,
Accusing him, instead,
Of a crime: "Gawain, you killed   4760

My lord, striking at him
Without any warning. May you
Be shamed, despised, and condemned,
Labeled as the traitor you are!
And all of Arthur's barons   4765
Know these words to be true."
Hearing this, my lord
Gawain leapt up, deeply
Shamed, but Agrevain
The Proud, his brother, stopped him: 4770
"For the love of God, good lord,
Don't dishonor your family!
I swear to defend you against
This knight and all the shame
Of these dishonorable claims."   4775
Said Gawain, "I will defend
Myself, with no one's help:
No one else should act,
Since I'm the one who's accused.
If in fact I'd done wrong   4780
To this knight, and knew I'd done wrong,
I'd very gladly seek
To make both peace and such
Amends as would please all
His friends and all of mine.   4785
But since he has chosen to insult me,
I will defend myself—
Here, or wherever he likes."
His accuser answered that in forty
Days, before the king   4790
Of Escavalon (more handsome,
I think, than Absalom),

He'd prove that Gawain was guilty
Of cruel and villainous treachery.
"As for me," said Gawain, "I swear   4795
To come riding right behind you,
And then we'll see who's right!"
    As soon as Guinganbresil
Left, my lord Gawain
Prepared to hurry after him.   4800
Knights with first-rate shields
And lances, helmets and swords,
Offered to lend them, but Gawain
Wanted only his own
Weapons. He rode off with seven   4805
Squires, seven horses,
And two shields. Taking leave
Of the court was a sad affair:
They beat their breasts, tore
Their hair, scratched their faces!   4810
No lady was able to hold back
An outflow of sorrow, but men
And women both wept. Yet Gawain
Had to go, and he went.
And now I'll tell you the adventures   4815
He found along the way.
    First, he met a group
Of knights riding through wooded
Country. He called to a squire
Following after them, all   4820
Alone, his right hand holding
The reins of a Spanish horse;
A shield was hung round his neck:
"Squire, tell me: who are

These knights?" The squire answered,   4825
"That one, sir, is Meliant
Of Lis, most worthy, most famous."
"And do you serve him?" "No sir,
I don't. My lord is Traé
Of Anet, second to no one."   4830
"By God," said Gawain, "I know
Traé very well indeed.
Where is he going? Don't hold back
Anything." "To a combat,* sir,
Which Meliant of Lis has arranged   4835
Against Tibault of Tintagel—
And you'd be welcome, I'm sure,
If you joined those in the castle."
"Lord," said Gawain, "wasn't
Meliant raised in Tibault's   4840
House? That's his foster father."
"May God save me, sir,
Yes. His father so loved
His vassal Tibault that as
He lay on his deathbed, he commended   4845
His little son to his care.
And Tibault protected and raised him
With as much affection as anyone
Could want, until young Meliant
Fell in love with Tibault's   4850
Daughter, who told him he couldn't
Have her love until

---

* *Tornoiement* in the twelfth century meant (1) modern "tournament"
or (2) serious, sometimes bloody combat. Here both meanings apply,
and the second needs to be stressed; see lines 4895-96, below.

He'd become a knight. And Meliant,
Wanting her very badly,
Went and became a knight.   4855
But when he pressed her, once more,
She said, 'By God, no,
That never will happen until
You stand before me so full
Of tournaments won, and battles,   4860
That you've paid the price for my love:
Whatever can be had for nothing
Is never as satisfying
Or sweet as what one must pay for.
Arrange a combat against   4865
My father, if you want my love,
For I need to know without
Any doubt that my love is worthily
Given before I can grant it.'
      "So Meliant did as she wanted,   4870
And arranged the combat, for Love
Enjoys such absolute power
On those in its grip that they never
Dare refuse Love
Whatever it wants them to do.   4875
And you, good sir, could not
Do better, in choosing which side
To fight on, than decide to help
Those in the castle, for they need you."
Then Gawain said, "Go on,   4880
My friend; rejoin your lord,
And leave the rest to me."
So the squire went on his way,
And Gawain went on his.

He was riding toward the castle,   4885
There being no other road.
Tibault had brought together
All his knights and his neighbors,
And sent for all his cousins,
Humble or great, young   4890
Or old, and his cousins had come.
But no one in Tibault's castle
Wanted the vassal to accept
A combat against his lord,
Terribly afraid that Meliant   4895
Intended to kill them all.
They'd walled up every entrance
To the castle, and made it a stronghold,
Blocking the doors with quarried
Stone, cemented in place,   4900
Leaving only a little
Gate, just that single
One, for going in
Or out—and that door wasn't wood,
But hammered from copper, made   4905
To last forever, and locked
By a bar forged of enough
Iron to have built a cart with!
And Gawain headed straight
For that door, with all his equipment,   4910
Having no choice: he either
Went through or else he went back.
The only other route
Would cost him a week of riding.
Finding the door locked,   4915
He crossed a fenced-in meadow

Close beside the tower,
Then dismounted under an oak tree
From which he hung his shields,
So the people in the castle could see them.   4920
Now most of those in the castle
Were glad the combat was postponed.
There was one old knight, brave
And experienced, of ancient lineage,
Rich in wisdom and land,   4925
And whatever he said was law:
No one disputed his judgment
Or refused to follow his advice.
He'd watched the strangers approach,
For they'd let themselves be seen   4930
From far off, even before
They reached the fence. And he said
To Tibault, "By God, my lord,
Unless my eyes deceive me
I see two of King Arthur's   4935
Knights arriving down there.
Two knights can accomplish a lot,
For one can win a tournament.
It seems to me, my lord,
That this is now a combat   4940
You can safely allow to begin,
For you've plenty of worthy knights,
And good soldiers, and sharp-shooting archers
Who can kill their horses under them—
For surely they'll need to fight   4945
Right here in front of this door.
Let them, if pride leads them on,
For the gain will all be ours,

And theirs will be the loss."
Tibault accepted this   4950
Advice, allowed his knights
To arm themselves, and those
Who wished to ride out of the castle.
And the joyful knights ordered
Squires to bring out armor   4955
And saddle horses, and the ladies
And girls hurried up
To the castle's highest places,
In order to watch the fighting,
And they clearly saw, beneath them,   4960
My lord Gawain's shields.
It seemed to them, at first,
Seeing a pair of shields
Hung from the oak tree's branches,
That two knights had come,   4965
And happy to have climbed so high,
Thinking themselves in luck,
Looking down and seeing
These two knights make ready.
     But only some of them thought so.   4970
Others were saying, "Good Lord
In Heaven! That knight down there
Has so many horses and so much
Equipment he could surely outfit
Two, but there's no one with him!   4975
Why does he need two shields?
Who's ever seen a knight
Carrying two shields at once?"
It struck them as wonderfully strange,
Seeing a single knight   4980

With more than the shield he needed.
As they were talking, knights
Began to emerge from the castle,
And Tibault's oldest daughter,
Who had brought about this combat,   4985
Stood at the top of the tower.
Her younger sister was with her,
Whose sleeves were always so elegant
That everyone called her the Girl
With the Narrow Sleeves, for they clung   4990
So closely to her arms. These two
Young ladies and a host of women
And girls had climbed as high
As they could, and clustered there, watching.
Knights quickly assembled   4995
In front of the castle. And none
Among them was worthy of so much
Attention as Meliant of Lis,
According to the girl he was courting,
Who said to the women around her,   5000
"Ladies, I must tell you
I've never seen such a knight—
It's the truth, and I have to say it—
As Meliant of Lis.
Isn't it wonderfully pleasant   5005
To watch such a man? He sits
His saddle so well, and he carries
His shield and his lance so beautifully,
With such ease and assurance."
But her sister, seated beside her,   5010
Observed that others looked better,
And the older sister was so angry

That she rose, intending to strike her.
But the other women held her
Back just long enough 5015
So the blow never landed—which made
The older sister still angrier.
Then the fighting began, down below them,
And many broken lances
And heavy sword-blows, falling 5020
On many knights, reminded
Them all of the high cost
Of fighting with Meliant of Lis:
No one wanted to remain
His opponent very long, 5025
For he drove them to the ground, and smashed
Their lances, and beat them with his sword.
No one on either side
Was fighting as well, and he made
His belovèd so happy that she couldn't 5030
Keep herself from saying,
"Ladies, ladies! What wonders!
Surely, you've never seen
The like, or heard of it, either!
He's easily best and most handsome 5035
Of all the men down there."
But her sister said, "I see
One who seems to me better."
The older sister turned
And said, exceedingly angry, 5040
"Slut! How dare you, miserable
Creature that you are, mutter
Foul-mouthed words and criticize
Anyone I choose to praise!

Here's something for your cheek—and try   5045
To be more careful, in the future!"
Then she slapped the younger girl
So hard that, clear and distinct,
Her face displayed the prints
Of each and all five fingers.   5050
The ladies around them drew
The young girl away, and scolded
Her sister, and immediately turned
To gossiping about Gawain.
"Lord," said one of the young ones,   5055
"That knight under the oak tree:
What's holding him back?" Another
Girl, speaking less carefully,
Declared he had sworn off fighting,
And then a third one said,   5060
"He must be a merchant. Let's leave him
Out of our conversation.
He's here to sell his horses."
"He's a moneychanger," said a fourth.
"And he doesn't think he can sell   5065
These poor knights, today, any
Of the goods he's brought along.
I'm telling the truth: those saddle-
Bags and boxes are stuffed
With money and silver cups."   5070
"Really," said the younger sister,
"You have wicked tongues—and you're wrong.
Could any merchant lift
The huge lance he's carrying?
These things you're saying are exceedingly   5075
Painful for me to hear.

I swear by the Holy Ghost
He seems a better fighter
Than a merchant or moneychanger.
He looks like a knight, and he is one."   5080
Then all the ladies spoke
In chorus, "Ah, dear sweet child,
Looking is not the same
As being: he imitates
The appearance, but all he wants   5085
Is to keep from paying a merchant's
Taxes. It's a bad mistake,
Because the inspectors will catch him
And put him in prison like the thief
And wicked scoundrel he is.   5090
He'll end up swinging by a rope!"
          But my lord Gawain could hear
Perfectly clearly every
Word these ladies were saying,
And he felt both angry and shamed.   5095
It seemed to him, and correctly,
He was being accused of treason,
And needed to defend himself.
If he held aloof from this battle
That others had agreed to fight,   5100
He would himself be dishonored,
And all his lineage with him.
And yet, not wanting to join
The fighting, for fear of being
Injured or captured, he held back,   5105
Though seeing how fierce the fighting
Remained, not slackening all day long,
He wished he were able to fight.

Now Meliant called for heavier
Lances, for striking better   5110
Blows. Till evening the fighting
Raged, outside the gates.
Whatever anyone won
Would be brought to some safer place.
The ladies saw a tall   5115
Squire, quite bald, carrying
The stump of a lance and wearing
A horse's harness on his shoulder.
And one of the ladies mocked him,
Calling out, "As God   5120
Is my witness, you've got to be
The craziest squire on earth,
Walking around in that throng
Collecting spearheads and harnesses,
And the stub-ends of lances, as if   5125
You knew what a squire should be doing!
Throw them away! They're worthless!
But I see from up here some pretty
Fancy goods just waiting,
Unguarded, for someone to take them.   5130
You're out of your mind, ignoring
When opportunity knocks.
And just look at that knight—the most cheerful
Fool ever born:
You could pluck out every hair   5135
In his mustache and he'd never move!
Make yourself rich! Hurry!
Go get it, if you've got any brains—
He won't try to stop you!"
So the squire went and whacked   5140

One of Gawain's horses
With his lance-stump, and said, "Fellow,
What's wrong with you, spending
The whole day lazing around,
Doing nothing but taking   5145
Care that your shield won't get scratched
And your lance doesn't get broken?"
"Go away," said Gawain. "It's none
Of your business. Someday, perhaps,
You'll know why I'm staying here.   5150
But it's none of your affair,
And I'm in no mood to tell you.
Go do whatever you ought
To be doing, and leave me alone!"
And the squire immediately left,   5155
Not being the sort who'd argue
With someone who spoke like Gawain.
      Then combat stopped for the day.
Many knights had been captured,
And many horses killed;   5160
The men from the castle had been braver,
But those outside had won
More booty. And as they parted
They agreed to return in the morning
And fight the whole day long.   5165
      So darkness finished the fighting,
And those who'd emerged from the castle
Went back inside. And my lord
Gawain followed along
Behind them, and in front of the door   5170
Met the brave old knight
Who, earlier that day, had advised

The lord of the castle to let
The combat begin. And speaking
With great politeness, he invited   5175
Gawain to spend the night
With them: "Good sir, your lodgings
Await you, here in this castle.
Stay with me, if you please,
For if you decide to ride on,   5180
There's nothing fitting nearby.
Do stay with me, my lord."
"Thank you, good sir, I will,"
Said Gawain, "and gladly. I've heard
Much less friendly words,   5185
Today." The old knight showed him
The way, talking of this
And that, then asked why,
With such a combat occurring,
He hadn't thought to join in.   5190
And Gawain told him the reason,
Explaining he'd been accused
Of treachery, and had to avoid
Becoming a captive, or wounded,
Or injured, until he'd proved   5195
Himself not guilty of that crime.
He and all his friends
Would find themselves dishonored,
Should he be late for the pre-
Arranged judicial combat.   5200
The old knight agreed,
And thought even better of Gawain:
If that was why he'd stayed
On the sidelines, he'd done the right thing.

Then he led Gawain to his house, 5205
And they both dismounted. But others
Inside the castle were not
So friendly, harshly accusing
Gawain, maintaining that Tibault
Should not have permitted him in. 5210
And Tibault's oldest daughter,
For sheer dislike of her sister,
Ingeniously argued the case:
"Believe me, nothing's been lost
Today, my lord. Indeed, 5215
It seems to me you've won
Far more than you think you have,
And I'll tell you exactly why.
All you have to do
Is order the arrest of a man 5220
Who instead of offering us help
Has wickedly tricked and deceived us,
Bringing into this castle
A load of lances, and shields,
And leading behind him horses. 5225
Pretending to be a knight,
He's cheating us out of taxes,
For all he really intends
To do is sell his goods.
But treat him as he deserves. 5230
Garin, Berte's son, has given him
Lodging right under your nose.
They've just gone by: I saw
Garin leading him home."
And thus she did whatever 5235
She could to dishonor the knight.

And her father mounted his horse,
Determined to see for himself.
He rode straight to the house
Where he knew Gawain could be found.   5240
Seeing her father ride out,
The younger sister left
As well, but by a back door,
For she wanted no one to see her.
She went, by another way,   5245
To the place where Gawain was lodging,
The house of Garin, Berte's son,
Who had two beautiful daughters.
And seeing their lord's young daughter
Coming, these girls were delighted,   5250
Nor made the slightest attempt
To conceal their pleasure. One took
Her right hand, and one the left,
Then led her happily in,
Kissing her eyes and her mouth.   5255
Their father, who was neither feeble
Nor poor, was already back
On his horse, and with his son,
Bertrand, was heading (as he often
Did) to court, there   5260
To confer with Tibault, his lord.
Meeting him in the middle of the street,
He greeted his lord, asking
Where he was going. And Tibault
Replied that, in fact, he was coming   5265
To Garin's own house. "That
Presents no problem whatever,"
Said Garin. "And, besides, now

I'll be able to show you the most
Handsome knight on earth."   5270
"Oh lord, that's not why I'm coming,"
Said Tibault. "I mean to arrest him.
He only pretends to be
A knight. He's really a merchant."
"Oh God!" cried Garin. "What wicked   5275
Words you've spoken! I am
Your man, and you are my lord,
But here and now, in the name
Of myself and all my family,
The moment you do such a thing,   5280
And in my very own house,
I'll deny your rule forever."
"As God is my witness," said his lord,
"That's not what I meant to do.
You and your house will have   5285
Nothing but honor at my hands.
All the same, I assure you,
Serious accusations
Have surely been made!" "Thank you,"
Said the old knight. "In which case,   5290
I'll be honored to have you visit
Both my house and my guest."
Side by side they rode
Together, quickly reaching
The old knight's house, where my lord   5295
Gawain had his lodging. Seeing them
Come, Gawain—a model
Of proper, courteous manners—
Greeted and welcomed them. The lord
And his vassal dismounted and greeted   5300

Gawain, and sat beside him.
      Then Tibault, lord of that castle,
Politely inquired Gawain's
Reason for merely watching
Their combat, all that day,   5305
Instead of joining in.
Without denying his actions
Were strange, and could have been shameful,
Gawain replied by explaining
That he had been accused   5310
Of treachery and had to defend
Himself at a king's court.
"An honest and faithful reason,"
Said Tibault. "No question about it.
Where will this combat take place?"   5315
"My lord," said Gawain, "at the king
Of Escavalon's court, and I'd better
Go directly there."
"I'll give you an escort," said Tibault,
"Who will show you the way. And since   5320
It's barren country you'll be crossing,
I'll make it easier by giving
You food to carry with you,
And horses on whose backs to put it."
But my lord Gawain replied   5325
He needed to bring nothing,
For he could buy whatever
He wanted, and where he was going
There'd be good horses and plenty
Of food and other supplies.   5330
So he'd ask nothing of Tibault.
      Tibault and his host made ready

To leave—but Tibault suddenly
Saw his younger daughter,
Who knelt in front of Gawain,   5335
Grasped him by the leg, and said,
"My lord, hear me, please!
I've come to complain against
My older sister, who struck me.
I beg you to set things right!"   5340
Gawain said nothing, not knowing
Her or what she meant,
But set his hand on her head.
Clasping his hand, she went on:
"My complaint about my sister,   5345
For whom I have no love,
Is directed to you, good sir,
Because she shamed me on your
Account." "But what can I do?"
He answered. "How can I help you?"   5350
Tibault, who had said his farewells,
Heard what the girl was asking,
And said, "My daughter, what business
Have you, complaining to this knight?"
And Gawain asked him, "My lord,   5355
Is this girl truly your daughter?"
"Indeed," said Tibault. "But pay
Her words no attention whatever.
She's an ignorant child, who knows nothing."
"Ah," said Gawain, "but I   5360
Would be unbearably cruel
If I simply ignored her words.
Tell me, my sweet and charming
Child, and tell me clearly,

What has your sister done wrong,   5365
And how can I set it right?"
"My lord, all you need
To do for me, tomorrow,
Is to bear arms in combat."
"But tell me, my sweet little friend,   5370
Have you ever asked for help
From any other knight?"
"No, sir." "Pay no attention,"
Said her father, "to anything she says.
Don't encourage her folly."   5375
But Gawain answered, "Sir,
God help me, but your daughter speaks
Extremely well for a girl
Of such tender years. How
Could I refuse such a claim?   5380
Indeed, just as she asks,
Tomorrow I'll fight in her name."
"Oh dear sweet sir, thank you!"
Said the girl, so overjoyed
That she bowed right to the ground.   5385
          And then they said no more.
The father rode off, with the girl
Seated on his horse in front of him,
And he asked his daughter to tell him
How this quarrel had begun.   5390
And she told him the truth, recounting
The tale blow by blow,
Explaining, "Sir, it made me
Unhappy, hearing my sister
Say that Meliant of Lis   5395
Was the best and most handsome of all,

For I saw, in the meadow below,
This noble-looking knight,
And I couldn't keep myself
From contradicting my sister   5400
By saying I saw someone better,
And then my sister called me
A stupid slut and pulled
My hair. And the devil with those
Who laughed! I'll let them cut   5405
My hair down to the nape
Of my neck, and spoil my looks,
If only this knight will take
To the field, tomorrow, and flatten
Meliant of Lis—   5410
And then, finally, my sister
Will have to hold her tongue!
All the ladies grew tired
Of her noise, today, but a little
Rain will wash away   5415
A big wind." "My daughter," he said,
"I hereby give you permission
To send him, as a sign of affection
And for courtesy's sake, a sleeve
From your dress, or perhaps a scarf."   5420
And she answered, in all innocence,
"Gladly, father, since you ask it.
But my sleeves are so terribly small
I wouldn't dare send one.
He might very well think   5425
I meant to insult him." "Daughter,
I'll take that into account.
You need say nothing more:

Everything is taken care of."
     And thus discussing the matter,   5430
He brought her home in his arms
And how happy it made him feel,
Holding her closely against him.
But when the older sister
Saw the younger returning   5435
In his arms, her heart was sore,
And she said, "Sir, where
Has she been, the Girl with the Narrow
Sleeves? What schemes and tricks
She invents—and she's started so soon!   5440
Where did you find her today?"
"And what are *you* trying to
Accomplish?" he answered. "You'd do well
To be silent: she's better than you are—
You, who've pulled her hair   5445
And struck her, which makes me angry.
You haven't acted well."
Hearing such scathing, scolding
Words from her father left her
Abashed and deeply distressed.   5450
And then the father took
Rich red silk from his strongbox,
And immediately had them make
A great wide sleeve. And then,
Calling his younger daughter,   5455
He told her, "Daughter, tomorrow
You're to rise early and go
To the knight's lodging before he
Leaves. Give him this sleeve
As a sign of affection, and he   5460

Can wear it when he comes to the combat."
And she assured her father
She'd be up at the crack of dawn,
Exactly as he wished, dressed
And ready to perform her errand.   5465
      With these instructions, her father
Left her, and the girl, extremely
Happy, ordered all
Her maids not to let her
Lie in bed, the next morning,   5470
But to wake her up at once
(If they wanted her to love them)
At the first light of day.
They said they were glad to obey,
And the very moment they saw   5475
The sun's first rays they came
And woke her, and helped her dress.
      She rose at dawn the next day
And went, all by herself,
To my lord Gawain's lodgings.   5480
But she hadn't come so early
That the household wasn't already
Awake and gone to church,
Anxious to attend Mass,
So the girl was obliged to wait   5485
A long time, at Garin's
House, while they finished their prayers
And heard all they needed
To hear. When they finally returned,
She threw herself in front   5490
Of Gawain, and said, "May God
Save you and give you joy!

Please, for love of me,
Wear this sleeve I bring you."
"Gladly, my dear," said Gawain,   5495
"And thank you very much."
But the knights could not linger long,
Needing to put on their armor;
They assembled in a group outside
The gates, ready to fight.   5500
And once again all
The ladies climbed the tower,
And watched brave and worthy
Knights forming their ranks.
And Meliant of Lis   5505
Was the first to come charging up,
Leaving those on his side
Hundreds of yards behind him.
And the older sister, seeing
Her lover, couldn't keep silent,   5510
But cried out, "Ladies, see!
Here comes the pride and glory
Of knightly chivalry!"
And Gawain spurred his horse
Directly at him, as fast   5515
As the beast could run, and Meliant
Met him. But his lance shattered,
And my lord Gawain struck him
So fierce a blow that Meliant
Was hurt, and fell to the ground,   5520
And Gawain grasped his horse
By the reins and handed them over
To a squire, directing that the beast
Be brought to the girl for whom

He was fighting. "Tell her I send   5525
This horse as her first prize
Of the day, and hope she approves."
And the squire quickly led
The horse, all saddled, to the girl,
Who'd already seen, from the high   5530
Tower window where she sat,
How Meliant of Lis had fallen.
And she said, "Now see, sister,
That Meliant of Lis, whom you've praised
So much, is stretched out flat   5535
On his back. How you've wasted your words!
But this proves what I told you, yesterday;
Judge for yourself, as God
Is my witness, which knight is better!"
It was hardly spoken by accident,   5540
For she meant to provoke her sister,
Who nearly lost her mind,
Screaming, "Slut, be quiet!
If I hear you say another
Word, I'll give you such   5545
A slap that you won't be able
To walk!" "God save us!"
Said the younger sister. "I've simply
Spoken the truth; there's no
Reason to hit me. By God,   5550
I saw him knocked to the ground,
And you were sitting right here,
And as far as I can tell
He's still not able to stand.
And even if it makes you angry,   5555
I have to say that every

Lady in this tower saw him
Knocked flat, with his legs in the air."
The older sister was ready
To strike, if only they'd let her,   5560
But all the ladies around them
Stopped her from hitting her sister.
Just then, they saw the squire
Coming, his right hand leading
The horse. He saw the young girl   5565
At the window, and presented her prize.
The girl thanked him sixty times
Over, asking that he tend
The horse and convey her thanks
To his lord, who was surely destined   5570
To be the master of this combat,
For every knight who encountered
His lance—so great was his skill—
Would say goodbye to stirrups
And saddle. Gawain had never   5575
Collected so many horses!
That day he presented four,
Each of them won at his hands:
The first he sent, as we've seen,
To Tibault's youngest daughter;   5580
The second went to Garin's
Wife, who was mightily pleased;
One of Garin's daughters
Got the third, the other the fourth.
Then fighting was over for the day,   5585
And the knights of the castle returned,
But Gawain carried with him
The day's highest honors,

Despite leaving the combat
Before the day was half over.   5590
And as he rode back to his lodgings
So many knights rode with him
That the way was packed with horses
And men, and all who saw him
Wondered, and asked, who   5595
He was, and where he'd come from.
Tibault's younger daughter
Met him in front of the house,
And all she could think of doing
Was to take him by the stirrup   5600
And greet him, using these words,
"Thank you, thank you, my lord!"
He realized what she meant
To say, and replied, frankly,
"Girl, I'd have to be old   5605
And gray before I refused
To serve you, wherever I might be.
If ever I hear that you need me,
From no matter how far away,
Nothing will keep me from coming   5610
The very first time you call."
"Many thanks," said the girl.
They chatted of this and that,
And then her father arrived,
Seeking to persuade Sir Gawain   5615
By any means he could
To spend the night at his house.
But Gawain excused himself,
Assuring Tibault that he could not
Stay. And then the lord   5620

Of the castle asked his name.
"Sir, I am called Gawain.
I never conceal my name
When anyone asks it, just
As I never tell it unless   5625
Someone bothers to ask."
And when Tibault heard that this
Was my lord Gawain, his heart
Filled with joy, and he said,
"Sir, do come and accept   5630
My house as your lodging for tonight,
For, let me tell you, never
In my life have I seen a knight
I so much wanted to honor,
And I've not been able to serve you."   5635
And he asked, again, if Gawain
Would stay, but Gawain persisted,
Refusing all invitations.
And then the girl, neither
A fool nor wicked, bent   5640
And kissed his foot, and commended
Him to Our Lord in Heaven.
And when Gawain asked her what
This gesture was intended to mean,
She answered by saying she'd kissed   5645
His foot, as she had, so he
Would never be able to forget her,
On account of this mark of special
Attention, wherever he went.
Then Gawain said, "Don't worry,   5650
My pretty friend: as God
Is my witness, I'll never forget you,

No matter where I may be."
          And then he said farewell
To Garin and all the others,   5655
Who commended him to God.
That night my lord Gawain
Took lodging at a monastery,
And found there whatever he needed.
And then, all the next day,   5660
He rode along the road
Until he saw a herd
Of does grazing at the edge
Of a dense wood. Calling
To his squire to stop where they were,   5665
He told him to bring the horse
He was leading (the very best
Gawain had) and a strong
Straight spear he was carrying as he went,
Then give his master the spear   5670
And the horse, taking in exchange
The reins of the palfrey Gawain
Had been riding. The squire quickly
Did exactly as instructed,
Bringing both horse and lance,   5675
And Gawain rode toward the deer,
Craftily approaching close
Enough to surprise a white
Doe, feeding near a blackberry
Thicket, and strike it on the neck.   5680
But the doe leapt away,
Exactly as a stag might have done,
And Gawain galloped after
And would have caught the fleeing deer

Except that his horse lost   5685
A shoe from a front foot.
Gawain turned to go back
To the road, where his squire was waiting,
But feeling his horse limping
He felt immense concern,   5690
Not knowing what might be hurting—
Perhaps it had bumped its hoof
On a tree stump? He told his squire
To dismount from his own horse
And find out what was wrong,   5695
For by now the horse was limping
Badly. The squire obeyed,
Lifted the horse's foot,
And found that the shoe was missing.
"My lord," he said, "we need   5700
A blacksmith. You have no choice
But to ride on gently until
We find one and this hoof is re-shod."
So on they went, until
They saw men leaving a castle.   5705
Those leading the way
Were wearing short clothes—boys
On foot, with packs of dogs.
And then came huntsmen, carrying
Sharpened spears. And then   5710
Came archers and men at arms,
Bearing bows and arrows.
And then came the knights.
And after the knights came a mounted
Pair, one of whom   5715
Was a boy in his teens, and the loveliest

Boy in the world. He
Alone greeted Gawain,
Taking him by the hand
And saying, "Sir, I've caught you.   5720
Go back the way I've just come
And let me offer you lodging.
Surely, it's now the hour
For resting, if you've no objections.
I have a courteous sister   5725
Who'd be very happy to see you,
And this gentleman riding with me
Will gladly show you the way.
Sir," he told his companion,
"I send you to go with this lord   5730
And lead him to my sister. Greet her,
First, and then give her
This message: tell her that by
The love and trust that she and I
Share, as brother and sister,   5735
If ever she has loved a knight
She must love this one, and treat him
Well, exactly the way
She'd treat me, her very own brother.
Let her offer him comfort   5740
And company, unless she objects,
Until we return from our hunt.
And when you see he's been welcomed
With all my sister's charm,
Come hurrying back to me,   5745
For I would like to seek
His company, too, and return
As soon as I possibly can."

And then the companion left,
Bringing my lord Gawain   5750
To a place where everyone hated him.
Gawain suspected nothing;
He'd never been there before
And knew no reason to be on
His guard. He noted how the castle   5755
Stood on an arm of the sea,
And saw how the tower and walls
Were so strong that nothing could shake them.
And everywhere he looked
He saw singularly beautiful people,   5760
And those who dealt in gold
And silver, and their coin-covered tables,
And saw shops and streets
Crowded with all sorts of workers
Plying their different crafts,   5765
Everything under the sun:
Mail-coats over here, and helmets;
Lances over there, and coats
Of arms; and harnesses
And spurs, and lances and spears;   5770
Weavers of cloth, and finishers,
Those who card, and those
Who shear; smelters of silver
And gold; makers of beautiful
Things, goblets and cups   5775
And lovely enameled ware,
Rings and belts and clasps.
One could have said, and truly,
They held a fair every day,
So bursting with goods was the place—   5780

Beeswax, and dyes, and pepper,
Squirrel fur, and fox, and whatever
Men made for other men.
   He went and looked at everything,
Here and there, far   5785
And near, then came to the tower,
From which servants came running to remove
Their armor and take their weapons.
Leaving the servants, his escort
Took Gawain into the tower,   5790
Then led him by the hand straight
To his host's sister, to whom
He said, "My beautiful friend,
Your brother greets you, and sends you
This lord, and commands you to offer him 5795
All the honor and service you can.
He asks you not to be vexed,
But to do your duty with such
A good heart that this knight might be
Your brother and you his sister.   5800
Don't be reluctant to allow him
Whatever a man might want,
But be charming, gracious, and generous.
Reflect on these words, for I'm leaving:
I must return to the hunt."   5805
And the girl answered, exceedingly
Happy, "Blessings on him,
For sending me company like this!
No one who lends me so handsome
A man can hate me, and I thank him. 5810
My lord," said the girl to Gawain,
"Come sit over here, beside me.

Since you're so handsome and noble,
And my brother asks me to befriend you,
I find you a delightful companion."   5815
      And then his escort left him,
Unwilling to linger, and my lord
Gawain remained, not
In the least inclined to protest
At being alone with the girl,   5820
Who was both agreeable and lovely,
And had been so perfectly raised
That being alone with a man
Seemed no particular risk.
They spoke of love, of course—   5825
Indeed, had they spoken of anything
Else, they would have been fools.
      Gawain made amorous advances,
Swearing he'd be her knight
The whole rest of his life,   5830
And she said no to nothing,
But cheerfully gave what he asked.
Just then, alas! a knight
Appeared, who spoiled their fun,
For he knew who Gawain was.   5835
He found them exchanging kisses,
Profoundly pleased with each other.
But seeing what they were up to
He couldn't hold his tongue,
But cried as loud as he could,   5840
"Shame on you, woman! Shame!
May God blast you to nothingness,
Allowing the very man
You ought to hate the most

To hug and kiss you like that,   5845
Happy to hold you in his arms!
You stupid, wicked woman,
Born to become such a slut!
Your hands should rip out his heart,
Not your foolish mouth.   5850
If your kisses struck to his heart
They could have pulled the heart
Right out of his belly—but your hands
Could do it better. And that
Is what you ought to have done,   5855
If a woman can do anything right.
But women are worthless creatures:
A woman who hates evil
And loves good is not
A woman, for she loses that name   5860
The moment there's good in her heart.
But you're a woman, all right,
To sit there, next to the man
Who killed your father, kissing him!
When a woman can have what she wants,   5865
She cares about nothing else."
And then he ran out of sight,
Not waiting to see what my lord
Gawain might have to say,
And the girl fainted dead   5870
Away, and lay still a long time.
Gawain bent and lifted her
Up, blue and pale
From the fright she'd had. And when
She was conscious again, she exclaimed,   5875
"Oh, we're as good as dead!

I'm going to die on your
Account, and you because
Of me. All the common
People will be coming—you'll see!—   5880
Ten thousand or more will be massing
Right in front of this tower.
And yet, there are plenty of weapons,
And I'll have you in armor in a minute!
One knight who knows what he's doing   5885
Surely can defend this tower."
Worried as she was, she ran
And fetched weapons and armor.
And once he was fully equipped
Both she and my lord Gawain   5890
Were considerably less concerned,
Although there was still a problem,
For she hadn't found him a shield.
But he picked up a heavy chessboard
And said, "My dear, don't bother: 5895
This is all the shield I need."
He threw the chessmen to the ground;
They were carved of ivory, ten times
Heavier and harder than usual.
Now, whatever happened,   5900
He was sure he could hold the door
And the entrance to the tower, for belted
To his side he wore Excalibur,
The best sword ever made:
It could cut through iron as if   5905
It were wood. The angry knight
Had run outside, and found there,
Milling about, the mayor

And many notables, and a swarming
Horde of other townsfolk   5910
Who clearly hadn't been feeding
On fish, their bellies were so fat!
He ran to this crowd as fast
As he could, crying, "Gentlemen,
To arms! Let's catch this traitor   5915
Gawain, who killed our lord!"
"Where? Where?" they shouted.
"By God," he answered, "I found him—
Gawain himself, that traitor!—
Sitting there in our tower,   5920
Hugging and kissing our lady,
And she wasn't objecting—
She liked it, she wanted more.
Come with me, let's get him!
If we can hand him over   5925
To our lord, we'll have done a great service.
This traitor surely deserves
To be caught in the middle of his shame.
But we have to take him alive,
Because our lord, and rightly,   5930
Wants him alive, not dead.
Dead men have nothing to fear.
Rouse the whole town! Everyone!
Do your duty! All of you!"
The mayor was ready in a moment,   5935
And all the notables with him.
Ah, you should have seen
Those clowns picking up axes
And pikes! They grabbed up shields
Without straps, and gates, and baskets.   5940

The town crier called them
To arms, and everyone came,
The town bell ringing
To remind them not to stay home.
Every single rogue   5945
Snatched up a pitchfork or a flail
Or a hammer: they made more noise
Than a mob out hunting snails!
Children came running, too,
Carrying whatever they could.   5950
Oh, Gawain would get himself killed,
Absent help from Heaven!
            And then the girl, brave
As she was, got ready to fight.
But first she called to the crowd,   5955
"Ah, you scum! You foaming
Dogs! You dirty rascals!
What devil sent you here?
Ha! What are you after?
May God deprive you of all pleasure!   5960
In the name of the Lord, you'll never
Lay hands on this knight in here:
You won't be able to count
The people he'll chop up and kill!
He didn't use wings, and fly   5965
To this tower; he came by no tunnel.
My brother himself sent him
Here, and asked me to be his host,
And treat him with all the warmth
And affection I'd show to my brother.   5970
You think, when my brother commands me,
I'm some kind of slut, giving him

Company, pleasure, and comfort?
Believe it if you want to: go on!
But I've told you my only reason;   5975
Nothing worse was involved!
But you're behaving wildly,
You're shaming me, coming
To my bedroom door with drawn
Swords in your hands, none of you   5980
Certain why you're here,
And even if you were, not saying
A word to me, which is why
I tell you you're all scum!"
But while she was telling them off,   5985
They were whacking away at the door
With their axes, trying to force their way
In, and they split it in two.
But the inside porter, guarding
The gate, defended his post,   5990
Meeting them sword in hand,
And the first one who came paid
So huge a price of admittance
That no one dared to follow.
Anxious to stay alive,   5995
They were all afraid of losing
Their heads. Those who'd pressed forward
Hurriedly beat a retreat;
No one would stick out a hand
Or risk a single step.   6000
And the girl picked up the chessmen
Lying on the floor and threw them
Angrily into their faces.
Tucking up her skirt

And swearing like a fishwife,   6005
She told them she'd kill them all,
If she could, before they killed her.
          But the peasants refused to give up,
Swearing they'd pull the tower
Down on their heads, if they didn't   6010
Surrender. They both continued
To fight, throwing great chessmen.
Most of the mob retreated,
Unable to endure these missiles,
And began digging at the tower's   6015
Foundation, hoping it would topple
Down, for they didn't dare fight
At the door, so well defended.
And let me tell you, that door
Was low and exceedingly narrow,   6020
And even two men abreast
Could not have made their way through—
Which was why a single bold knight
Could hold and defend it so well.
For slicing these unarmored peasants   6025
From the top of their heads to their teeth,
They needed to call on no better
Porter than the one they had.
          Now the lord who'd offered Gawain
Lodging knew nothing of all this,   6030
Although he returned from the hunt
As soon as he possibly could.
Meanwhile, the peasant sappers
Kept attacking the tower.
And now (I don't know how)   6035
Guinganbresil also arrived;

He galloped up to the castle
And was shocked to the very bottom
Of his soul, seeing the assembled
Peasants hammering and digging.   6040
He had no idea, of course,
That Gawain was in the tower.
But the minute he understood it,
He warned the mob that no one
Who valued his life had better   6045
Be brave enough to touch
So much as a single stone.
His saying so wouldn't make
Them stop, they replied: if he
Were inside with Gawain, they'd pull   6050
The tower down on them both.
And seeing how little attention
They paid him, he thought he'd better
Go find the king, and let him
See the unholy mess   6055
These bourgeois men were making.
          So he found the king in the wood,
And informed him what was happening:
"My lord, the mayor and all
The merchants are heaping dishonor   6060
On your name. Ever since
This morning they've been attacking
Your tower. Make them sorry,
Make them pay, or I'll
Be shamed. I accused Gawain   6065
Of treachery, as you know quite well,
But the man to whom you've offered
Lodging in your house is Gawain

Himself. Because he accepted
Your offer, it's right and proper   6070
That now you give him protection."
The king gave Guinganbresil
This answer: "Master, the moment
I get there, there'll be no danger!
I'm terribly sorry, believe me,   6075
That something like this has happened.
The fact that my people hate him
So desperately doesn't displease me,
But having made him my guest,
Honor requires me to keep him   6080
Safe from all such assaults."
They rode straight to the tower
And found it surrounded by a howling
Mob of townsfolk. The king
Immediately commanded the mayor   6085
To order everyone away.
And the moment the mayor spoke,
They left, and no one lingered.
A wise old knight who'd been born
And raised in the town, and had given   6090
Advice that everyone welcomed—
Sensible and sane—said
To the king, "My lord, it's time
I gave you some heartfelt counsel.
It's hardly surprising that the man   6095
Guilty of murdering your father,
And accused of a treacherous killing,
Should come here and be attacked,
For everyone here hates him,
And hates him rightly, as you know.   6100

But once you've offered him lodging
You have no choice but to keep him
Safe from capture or harm.
And to tell you the whole truth,
He who is truly obliged   6105
To protect him is Guinganbresil,
Who came to Arthur's court
And accused the man of treachery.
This fact can't be denied:
Gawain came here to defend   6110
Himself. But I advise
A delay in any such combat,
And that Gawain be sent in search
Of the bleeding spear, its point
Forever dripping a single,   6115
Unstoppable drop of blood.
Either he brings you that lance,
Or else he returns and you lock him
Up, as he's locked up now.
There'd be better cause for keeping him   6120
In prison than you have right now—
And could you invent a jail
So severe it could hold a man
Like that forever? Besides,
Given the chance, you should make   6125
Your enemy suffer as much
As you possibly can. I doubt
I could tell you a better way
To torment this fellow Gawain."
          The king accepted this advice.   6130
He entered the tower, looking for
His sister, and found her still angry.

But she rose to greet him, as did
My lord Gawain—and he,
If he felt any fear, refused   6135
To show it by trembling or changing
Color. Guinganbresil
Came forward, greeting the girl,
Who'd become extremely pale,
Then speaking these empty words: 6140
"Oh Gawain, Gawain! Dear sir,
You had my safe conduct for coming
Here, provided only
That, intending to return alive,
You keep yourself from rashly   6145
Entering any of my lord's
Castles or towns. Under
The circumstances, there's nothing
To say about what you've done."
And then the wise old man   6150
Spoke up: "My lord, please God,
These matters may all be arranged.
To whom can one complain,
When merchants and butchers attack you?
One couldn't sort that out   6155
From now to the day of Last Judgment!
But here's what my lord the king,
Standing right here, proposes:
He's ordered me to suggest,
If you and he both agree,   6160
That this trial by combat should be
Postponed for another year,
And that you, Sir Gawain, should leave here,
Bound however by an oath

To my king, namely, that you'll   6165
Return, in no more than a year,
Bringing that lance dripping
Bright red blood—a spear,
It is written, which in time to come
Will destroy the entire kingdom   6170
Of Logres (already known
As the land of ogres). This
Is the pledge and agreement my lord
The king is seeking from you."
"Ha!" said Gawain. "I'd much   6175
Prefer to be murdered where I stand,
Or to spend eight years in prison,
Than to bind myself to such
A pledge, and swear to perform it.
I'm not so afraid of death   6180
That I wouldn't rather die
With honor than allow myself,
Living, to be perjured and shamed."
"Ah no, good sir," said the old man.
"No dishonor is involved,   6185
Nor any breaking of your word,
If you do as I instruct:
Swear to do your best
To find and bring back the lance.
If in the event you can't,   6190
Simply return to this tower
And your promise will be fulfilled."
"In that case," said Gawain, "I'm inclined
To accept the oath you propose."
A precious, holy relic   6195
Was quickly brought in, and the oath

Was solemnly recited: Gawain
Promised to do all he could
To find the bleeding lance.
            And so the battle between   6200
Gawain and Guinganbresil
Was postponed for the term of one year.
And Gawain escaped the great peril
Hanging over his head.
He immediately left the tower,   6205
Having said farewell to the girl
And ordered all his servants
To go back home, taking
Every one of the horses
With them, except Gringolet.   6210
His squires and pages wept,
Obliged to leave their lord,
But they went, and I've no interest
In describing any of their sorrow.
For now, this *Story of the Grail*   6215
Is done with my lord Gawain,
And will turn its attention to Perceval.
            And the book tells us that Perceval
Had so completely lost
His memory he'd even forgotten   6220
God. Five Aprils and five Mays
Had passed, five whole years,
And he'd never entered a church
To adore God or His saints.
For five years he lived   6225
Like this, but never gave up
Hunting chivalric adventure,
Engaging in the wildest exploits,

Savage and cruel and hard.
He hunted them, and found them, 6230
And proved his courage over
And over; nothing he started
Was ever left unfinished.
In those five years he sent
Fifty worthy knights 6235
To Arthur's court, as his prisoners.
       And so he spent five years
Without a thought of God.
And then, at the end of those years,
He found himself in a wilderness, 6240
Riding, as he usually rode,
Armored from head to foot,
When he met with five knights,
Along with ten ladies,
Their heads completely covered, 6245
And all were walking, not riding,
In woolen robes, and wearing
No shoes. Seeing him mounted
As he was, armored, with his shield
And his lance, all the ladies 6250
Doing penance for their sins,
Barefooted, striving for the good
Of their souls, were struck with astonishment.
Then one of the five knights
Stopped him, and said, "Good sir, 6255
Don't you believe in Jesus
Christ, who wrote the new Law
And gave it to Christians like us?
Surely it's wrong, and indeed
A great sin, to be bearing arms 6260

On the very day of His death."
Not knowing what day it was,
Or what time of day, or what year
(His heart so deeply troubled),
Perceval asked, "What day   6265
Is today?" "What? You don't know?
Today is Good Friday, when we openly
Honor the Cross, and weep
For the sins we've committed. Betrayed
For thirty pieces of silver,   6270
Christ was crucified today.
He who had never sinned,
But saw how the world was sinning,
Chose, of his own volition,
To take on human form.   6275
He was God and man in one,
Born of the Holy Virgin,
Conceived of the Holy Ghost—
God in flesh and blood,
Divinity covered by the skin   6280
Of a man: no one can doubt it.
Refuse to believe these things,
And you'll never see His face.
He was born of Our Lady, the Virgin,
Mingling His holy self   6285
With the soul and shape of a man,
And, indeed, on this very day
Was nailed to the Cross, and traveled
To Hell, and freed those who love Him.
He died the most saintly of deaths,   6290
Saving the lives of the living
And resurrecting the dead.

The Jews, in their wicked jealousy
(They ought to be killed like dogs!)*
Setting Him high on the Cross, 6295
Harmed themselves, but helped us,
For they were lost, and we
Were saved. Those who believe in
Him must give Him our penance,
This day; no believer 6300
Should wear armor or fight."
"And where have you come from?" Perceval
Asked. "From there, good sir,
In the midst of this forest, where a saintly
Hermit dwells—so holy 6305
A man, indeed, that he lives
Only by the glory of God."
"Tell me: what were you seeking?
What did you ask for? What
Did you do?" "What?" said a lady. 6310
"We asked forgiveness for our sins,
And confessed them all. Nothing
A Christian could ever do,
If he hopes to please his Lord,
Could possibly be more urgent." 6315
     Hearing these words, Perceval
Wept, and wanted to speak
With the holy hermit himself.

* Poirion claims that "the invective against the Jews is *surprisingly* violent" (p. 1371n, emphasis added) and translates *an devroit* tuer *come
chiens* as *on devrait les* abattre *comme des chiens,* although by 1150 *tuer*
meant "to kill" rather than "to strike." Says Father Edward H. Flan-
nery, "Medieval anti-Semitism left a mark on both Jew and Christian"
(*The Anguish of the Jews* [New York: Macmillan, 1964], 144).

"That's where I want to go,"
He said, "to this hermit, if only   6320
I knew which road to take."
"Sir, if you wish to see him,
All you need do is follow
The path that brought us here,
Straight through this dense forest,   6325
Paying careful attention
To the branches we tied together
With our own hands as we came.
We did this so no one seeking
The holy hermit could lose   6330
His way and fail to find him."
          They commended him to God
And asked him no more questions,
And Perceval followed their path,
Sighing from the bottom of his heart   6335
For all the sins against God
He'd committed, which he now repented.
He wept as he rode through the wood,
And when he arrived at the hermit's
Dwelling, he dismounted, and disarmed   6340
Himself. Tying his horse
To an elm tree, he entered the hermitage.
And there, in a tiny chapel,
He found the hermit, with a priest
And a choir boy (I tell it as it happened),   6345
Just beginning the most beautiful,
The sweetest service the sainted
Church can celebrate.
Perceval dropped to his knees
The moment he entered that chapel,   6350

But the holy hermit called to him,
Seeing the honest tears
Rolling down his cheeks
All the way to his chin.
And Perceval, deeply afraid   6355
Of having offended God,
Clasped the hermit's feet
And, bending low, his hands
Joined in supplication,
Begged for help, for his need   6360
Was great. The good man instructed
Him to make his confession,
For sins could not be forgiven
Before confession and repentance.
"Sir," said Perceval, "for five   6365
Full years I haven't known
Where I was, or believed in God,
Or loved Him. All I have done
Was evil." "Good friend," said the hermit,
"Tell me why this happened,   6370
And pray God to have mercy
On your sinful soul." "Sir,
Once I was at the Fisher King's
Castle, and I saw—without
Any question—the bleeding lance,   6375
And seeing that drop of blood
On the bright white of its point,
I never asked what or why.
There are no amends I can make.
And when I saw a holy   6380
Grail, I had no idea
For whom it was meant, and said nothing,

And ever since I've felt
Such sadness that I wished to die;
I forgot about God and never   6385
Prayed for his grace and mercy
Or did what I should to deserve it."
"Ah!" said the hermit. "Good friend,
Now you must tell me your name."
And he answered, "Perceval, sir."   6390
And hearing this, the hermit
Sighed, for he knew that name,
And said, "Brother, this comes
From a sin of which you know nothing.
It happened the day your mother   6395
Heard you say you were leaving,
And she fell to the ground in a faint,
Near the bridge, in front of the door,
And there she died of her sorrow.
And that was the sin which caused you,   6400
Later, to ask no questions
About the grail or the lance;
Everything followed from that.
You've only survived this long,
Believe me, because she commended   6405
You to our Holy Lord.
Her prayer had such spiritual strength
That for her sake God gave you
Protection from prison and death.
That sin stiffened your tongue   6410
When you saw, passing before you,
That spearpoint that goes on bleeding
And never asked what it was.
Not knowing for whom the grail

Was meant, you were out of your mind. 6415
He who was served is my brother:
Your mother was his sister, and mine,
And the rich Fisher King
Is the son, I believe, of the man
For whom the grail was intended. 6420
But don't imagine it holds
Salmon and pike and eels!
A single sacred wafer
Is all it contains, and it keeps him
Alive and gives him comfort, 6425
So holy a thing is that grail,
And he so exceedingly spiritual
That without the Eucharist he receives
From the grail he could not live.
It's been like this for fifteen 6430
Years: he never leaves
The room you saw the grail
Go to. I wish to administer,
Now, your penance for that sin."
"Oh my uncle, gladly!" 6435
Said Perceval. "With a willing heart!
My mother having been your sister,
I am truly your nephew, and you
My uncle, and well belovèd."
"Indeed, good nephew. Now repent! 6440
If you care for your soul as you should,
You'll open yourself to repentance.
The first thing you'll do each day,
The first place you'll go to, will be church,
Where soul and body will prosper. 6445
Never omit this, for any

Reason! Cathedral or chapel
Or parish church, go
As soon as the bells are rung,
Or, when you're awake, even sooner.   6450
The holy service won't hurt you,
And your soul will profit. If the priest
Has already begun to say Mass,
Remain there and hear the rest,
Listen to every word   6455
He either speaks or sings.
If your heart is sufficiently willing,
It's not too late: return
To grace, and then to Heaven!
Love God, adore Him, believe   6460
In Him. Honor good men
And women. Stand when the priest
Enters: it costs you little,
But truly God loves to see it
As the sign of a humble spirit.   6465
If a girl asks for your help,
Give it, and help yourself.
Or a widowed lady, or an orphan:
These are acts of absolute charity.
Help whom you can, as you should.   6470
Be careful, never fail them!
These are the things I wish you
To do, to reclaim God's grace
As, once, you used to have it.
Tell me: is your heart willing?"   6475
"Entirely willing," said Perceval.
"And now I'd like you to remain
With me for two whole days,

And in penitence dine with me,
Eating the foods I eat."   6480
And Perceval gave his consent,
And the hermit bent and whispered
A prayer in his ear, and had him
Repeat it till he knew it by heart—
A prayer full of the sacred   6485
Names God is known by,
His highest and holiest names,
Only to be invoked
When a man is in mortal fear.
Once he had learned it, the hermit   6490
Forbade him ever to say it
Except when facing the greatest
Danger. "Nor will I, sir,"
Said Perceval. And then he heard
Mass, and was filled with joy.   6495
And after the service he adored
The Cross, and wept for his sins,
Humbly repenting of them,
Over and over for a very
Long time. He dined, that night,   6500
Exactly as the hermit pleased,
On parsley, lettuce, and water-
Cress, and the bread they ate
Was baked of wheat and barley,
And they drank cold clear water.   6505
And his horse was fed on straw,
With a full basin of barley,
And he slept in a good dry stable,
Cared for as a horse requires.
          And Perceval learned, once again,   6510

That Our Lord had died that Friday,
Crucified high on the Cross.
He made his Easter communion
Humbly, in perfect simplicity.
   And here the story breaks   6515
Away from Perceval,
About whom the tale turns silent:
I'll speak a good deal of Gawain
Before Perceval is mentioned again.*
   Gawain had gone a long way,   6520
Once he'd escaped from the tower
Where the angry townsfolk trapped him.
In the latter part of the morning
He was galloping up a hill
When he came to an immense oak tree   6525
And saw the shade it provided.
And he saw a shield hung
From its branches, and a spear stuck
In the ground. He hurried over
To the oak, where he found a small   6530
Scandinavian palfrey,
Which struck him as very strange,
For shields and armor and weapons
Were ordinarily not
To be found with women's horses.   6535
Were it a stallion, he thought,
He could have concluded that a knight
In search of fame and fortune
Might have been crossing this country,

---

* In fact, in the remaining pages that Chrétien lived to write, we never
return to Perceval

And could have climbed this hill.   6540
Looking under the oak,
He saw a girl, who would have
Seemed lovely and charming, had she shown
Signs of happiness and joy.
But her hands were raised to her hair,   6545
As if to rip it out;
Her grief could not be mistaken.
And the cause of her grief was a knight
Over whom she was bent, covering
His eyes and his face and his mouth   6550
With kisses. As Gawain came closer
He saw the knight had been hurt,
His face cut to shreds,
A great deep sword wound
Right in the middle of his head   6555
And another along his side,
And blood spurting all over.
The wounded knight kept fainting,
Again and again, until
At last he slept. When Gawain   6560
Saw him, he could not tell
If the man were living or dead,
And asked, "Girl, is this knight
Likely to live?" And she answered,
"Sir, you can easily see   6565
How terribly badly he's wounded:
The least of these injuries could kill him."
"My sweet friend," he said,
"If you don't mind, please wake him,
For I wish to ask him about   6570
The state of affairs in this land."

"Sir," said the girl, "I will not
Wake him: I'd rather let
Myself be flayed alive,
For there's no one I've ever loved   6575
So much, and no one I will,
As long as I live. What a wicked
Fool I'd be, seeing him
At rest and asleep, to do
Anything that might annoy him."   6580
"Then I'll wake him myself, by God,"
Said Gawain, "because I need to."
Then turning his lance around,
He touched the sleeping knight's shoulder,
And woke him, but touched him so softly   6585
And gently that he did him no harm,
For which the wounded knight
Thanked him: "Sir, I offer you
Five hundred thanks for so
Politely waking me up   6590
That you caused me no pain whatever.
But let me beg you, on your own
Account, not to continue
Your journey. You'd be a fool.
Believe me, stay where you are."   6595
"Stay here, sir? But why?"
"By God, since you want to be told,
Sir, I'll tell you. No knight
Can ever come back, if he travels
In that direction, whether   6600
He keeps to the road or takes
To the open fields. There lies
The Galloway border: no one

Who crosses that border can ever
Return. Indeed, no one   6605
Ever has, except
For me, and you see my condition,
So badly hurt that, it seems
To me, I can hardly last
Till sunset. I encountered a knight   6610
Over there, so strong, so skilled,
So haughty, that no one I've ever
Met could possibly match him.
And that's why I tell you to leave,
Rather than continue down   6615
This hill. "By God," said Gawain,
"Running away is for peasants!
I didn't come here to turn back:
Whoever might want to call me
A coward could certainly do so,   6620
If I started in this direction,
Then turned around and went back.
I'll keep to this road, by God,
Until and unless I'm stopped."
"I see that you'll surely go on,"   6625
Said the wounded knight. "You crave
The honor and glory, and you'll seek them,
Whatever the cost. But if
You don't mind, if it's not too much,
Let me ask you, please,   6630
If God grants you that honor—
Though there's never been a knight
Who's earned it, and I think there never
Will be any such knight,
Neither you nor anyone else—   6635

That if you come back this way
You'd do me the favor of stopping,
Here, to see if I'm dead
Or alive, or better, or worse.
And if I'm dead, for charity's   6640
Sake, in the name of the Holy
Trinity, I beg you to care for
This girl and keep her from any
Misery or shame. And my reason
For asking is that God could never   6645
Make, and never will make
Again, a girl any nobler—
So open and generous, so courteous
And beautifully raised. Her sorrow
Now, is surely for me,   6650
For she sees me, as I am, near death."
My lord Gawain promised
That, absent his capture or another
Such obstacle, he would surely return
To this spot, and the wounded knight,   6655
And would give the girl whatever
Aid and counsel he could.
        And then he left them, and rode on
Through fields and forests, never
Stopping until he came to   6660
A strong castle, bordering
On the sea, with a port full of ships—
So towering a castle that it stood
As mighty as noble Pavia.
Spread out on the other side   6665
Were vineyards and a great city,
Clean and well kept and beautiful,

With a river than ran below it
And came lapping against its walls
Before it flowed to the sea.   6670
Both the castle and the town
Were guarded by tall stone walls.
My lord Gawain rode into
The city, across a bridge,
And when he arrived at the very   6675
Center of the place he saw,
In a courtyard, under a yew tree,
A girl standing alone
And staring at her image in a mirror,
And her skin was white as snow.   6680
And on her head she wore
A close-fitting golden crown.
Gawain spurred his ambling
Horse, to reach her sooner,
And she cried out, "Slowly, slowly,   6685
Good sir! Go gently! You're dashing
Ahead like a wild-tempered fool!
There's really no need for such haste:
Don't hurry your horse for no reason.
That's madness, good sir, plain madness."   6690
"God's blessings on you, young lady!"
Called out my lord Gawain.
"Now tell me, my pretty friend,
What did you think I was up to,
Riding toward you like that,   6695
Not knowing why I had come?"
"Oh yes, I knew, good knight,
I knew perfectly well."
"And my intention?" "Was to steal me

Away and carry me off,   6700
Draped on your horse's neck."
"Exactly, young lady, exactly!"
"I knew I was right," she said.
"But the devil with that sort of thing!
Don't think I plan to let you   6705
Cart me away on your horse.
I'm not some silly little girl
Who plays such games with you fellows,
Letting you lug me away
When you need to prove your knighthood.   6710
You won't hoist me up there!
But if you're a good enough knight,
I'll gladly go where you lead.
Just take the trouble, please,
To walk into that garden   6715
And find my palfrey; it's in there,
And I'll ride along behind you
No matter what troubles and problems,
What sadness and misery and misfortune
You experience, traveling with me."   6720
"Is courage all that's required,"
He asked, "my sweet young friend?"
"Fellow, as far as I know
That's all," the girl replied.
"Ah, my pretty, and what   6725
About my horse, if I go there?
Where will I leave him? He can't
Possibly cross on that plank."
"No indeed, sir, so leave him with me,
And you go walking across.   6730
I'll stay and watch your horse

For just as long as I'm able.
But hurry on back, if you can,
For who knows how long it can wait?
Perhaps it won't stay here in peace— 6735
Someone might lead it off
Before you come back." "Quite so,"
He said. "You're right. And if
It's led off, you'll be excused,
And the same if it somehow escapes: 6740
You won't hear me complaining."
        Then he gave her the horse, and went,
But had the good sense, at least,
To keep his armor and weapons,
In case there was someone there 6745
Who might want to stop him, keep him
From leading off the palfrey,
In which case he would have to fight
Before he could bring it back.
        Having crossed the plank 6750
He saw an immense mass
Of people watching in wonder,
And they all cried out, "Girl,
May you burn in Hell for the evil
You do! May bad things happen 6755
To someone with no respect
For the brave! Oh shame! You've caused
So many to have their heads
Cut off! And you, who bring her
Her horse, you simply don't know 6760
The miseries you're bound to suffer
If you put those reins in her hand!
Oh knight, why have you come?

Truly, you'd never be here
If you knew the dishonor, the misery,   6765
The misfortune and pain you'll experience
The moment you do what she wants!"
      Every one of them shouted
These things at Gawain, trying
To keep him from coming after   6770
The palfrey, trying to turn him
Back. He may have heard them,
But had no intention of listening:
He greeted them all, most politely,
And as they returned his greetings   6775
It seemed that all the spectators
Felt, in advance, great
Distress and sorrow for his fate.
Reaching the palfrey, my lord
Gawain stretched out his hand,   6780
Intending to grasp the reins
(For the horse was both bridled and saddled).
But a tall knight seated
Beneath a green-leaved olive tree
Spoke up: "Knight, you're wasting   6785
Your time, coming for that palfrey.
Just lay a finger on that horse
And you'll stand convicted of enormous
Arrogance. I will not try
To forbid you, I will not stop you,   6790
If you really want to take it.
But I'd advise you to leave:
Just stop in your tracks, or else
You'll encounter serious trouble."
"All the same, I won't stop,   6795

My good sir," said my lord Gawain,
"For the girl who was looking in her mirror,
Standing under that tree,
Sent me, and why would I come,
If I didn't intend to fetch her   6800
Her horse? I'd be labeled a liar
And coward all over the world."
"Good brother," the tall knight replied,
"You'll be getting more than you've asked for.
May God our Father witness,   6805
To whom I hope to surrender
My soul, that I've never seen
A knight do what you mean
To do without suffering
The pain of having his head   6810
Cut off. It will happen to you.
I've tried to warn you off
Without the slightest self-interest—
For let me assure you, you can lead
Away that horse without   6815
Interference from me or anyone
Else. But your path will be perilous
Once you presume to touch it.
Again, I advise you to stop
Before you lose your head."   6820
These words had no effect
On Gawain, who did not pause.
He led the palfrey, which had
A head part white, part black,
Back across the plank,   6825
Which it walked over easily, having
Learned on repeated trips

In both directions how to do it.
Then Gawain took it by the reins,
Which were made of silk, and led it   6830
Directly to the tree where he'd met
The girl staring at her mirror;
She'd let her cloak and her kerchief
Fall to the ground, the better
To show off both her face   6835
And her figure. My lord Gawain
Brought her the palfrey, bridle
And saddle and all, and said,
"Come over here, girl,
And I'll help you up on your horse."   6840
"By God," said the girl, "you'll never
Be able to boast, wherever
You go, that you held me in your arms.
If your naked hand so much
As touched anything I wore,   6845
Or brushed against my skin,
I'd be dishonored and stained.
What a misfortune, if anyone
Knew or said you were actually
Able to touch my flesh!   6850
I'd infinitely rather, believe me,
That here and now they cut
My skin and flesh to the bone!
Leave the palfrey to me:
Get back! By God, I know how   6855
To mount. I don't need your help.
May God allow me, today,
To see you have what I hope
You will have. It would give me great pleasure!

But wherever you happen to go,   6860
Never touch my clothes
Or my body: don't even come close!
I'll ride along behind you
Until I get to see you
Suffering pain, misfortune,   6865
And sorrow on my account,
And I know I'll see you twisting
And turning to get away,
But you're going to die in the end!"
      My lord Gawain listened   6870
To every word the haughty girl
Spoke, but made no reply;
He gave her the palfrey, and she
Gave him back his horse.
Then Gawain bent down, intending   6875
To take her cloak from the ground
Where she'd dropped it, and hand it to the girl,
Who only stared, neither
Afraid nor slow at heaping
Shameful abuse on a knight: 6880
"Fellow," she said, "what business
Of yours are my cloak and kerchief?
By God, I'm nowhere near
So naive as you think I am!
I've never asked you to offer   6885
Me service, nor do I want to:
Your hands aren't clean
Enough to handle my clothes,
Nor even touch my head.
Why do you have to grab at   6890
Whatever comes close to my eyes

And my face and my mouth? God's
Own Son couldn't stand the thought
Of you in my service, and neither
Can I. I've no interest whatever!"   6895
     And then, having put on her cloak
And her kerchief, she mounted her palfrey,
Exclaiming, "Knight, go
Wherever you feel like going,
And I'll follow behind you until   6900
I see you dishonored on my
Account—today, if it pleases
God." Gawain said nothing,
Not speaking a word. Completely
Shamed, he mounted and they left.   6905
Riding with his head bent low,
He headed for the great oak tree
Where he'd left the girl and the dying
Knight, whose injuries were such
That he desperately needed a surgeon.   6910
No one was better than Gawain
At the curing of all such wounds,
And seeing in a hedgerow an excellent
Herb, useful for the easing
Of pain, he went to pluck it.   6915
And as soon as he had it, he went straight
To the oak tree, where he saw the girl
Overwhelmed with sorrow;
The moment she saw him, she said,
"My very dear sir, I believe   6920
This knight of mine is dead,
For he hears and understands nothing."
Then my lord Gawain dismounted,

And felt the knight's pulse, and found it
Still strong; neither his mouth 6925
Nor his cheeks had gone cold. So he said,
"Girl, this knight is not dead,
But very much alive,
For his pulse and breathing are fine.
If none of his wounds is mortal, 6930
I've brought him an excellent herb
Said to be very helpful
At stopping much of the pain
And suffering his injuries have caused,
For according to all the books 6935
On these subjects nothing better
Has ever been found to put
On a wound. It's written that it has
Such strength, indeed, that simply
Applying it to the bark of infected 6940
Trees—not yet quite dry
And dead—will cause the roots
To grow again, and the trees
Will return to life, sprouting
New branches and leaves and flowers. 6945
You needn't worry about
Your lover dying, my dear,
Once this herb has been spread
On his wounds, and bandaged in place.
But I'll need a well-made kerchief 6950
To tie it on as I should."
"I'll give you one right away,"
She said with no hesitation,
"This one I've got on my head,
Since I have no other with me." 6955

She took the white and delicate
Kerchief off her head,
And Gawain tore it, as he had to,
In order to make a bandage
That would hold the herb in place,   6960
The girl offering him all
The help she knew how to give.
Then Gawain stood and watched
Until the knight sighed
And spoke: "May God reward   6965
Whoever restored my power
Of speech. I was very afraid
Of dying before I was able
To confess. Devils were already
Standing in line, waiting   6970
For my soul. Before my body is buried
I need to be confessed.
I know a priest, nearby,
And if I could find a horse
I could go and tell him all   6975
My sins, and make my confession,
And then receive communion.
I wouldn't fear death, after that,
For then I'd be in a state
Of grace, fully confessed.   6980
Do me this service, please,
If I'm not asking too much:
That squire, bouncing along
On his nag—may I use his horse?"
Hearing this, my lord   6985
Gawain turned round and saw
A squire approaching. Who

Was he? I'm going to tell you.
His hair was red, thick,
Stiff, and standing straight up   6990
Like a wild boar in anger,
As were his eyebrows, which seemed
To grow all the way down
His face, and over his nose,
Covering everything as far   6995
As his huge and twisted mustache.
His mouth was narrow, his heavy
Beard was forked and curly.
His neck was short, his chest
Immense. Gawain intended   7000
To greet him, asking if the knight
Could use his nag, but first
Spoke to the knight: "By God,
This squire is someone completely
Unknown to me. I'd rather   7005
Give you seven horses,
If I had them here, than that nag,
Such as it is." "Sir,
Believe me, all he wants
Is to injure you, if he can."   7010
Then Gawain stepped forward, facing
The onrushing squire, and asked him
Where he was going. And the squire,
Somewhat deficient in courtesy,
Replied, "Fellow, it's none   7015
Of your business where I come from
Or go, or what road I follow!
May misfortune fall on your head!"
My lord Gawain paid him

What he deserved, for these words,   7020
Striking such a blow,
With his open palm (gloved
For combat), that the squire fell over
Backward and tumbled to the ground.
He kept trying to rise,   7025
But instead—believe me!—dropped
On his face nine times over
(Or more), crawling on hands
And knees no farther than a spear-length.
When he could finally stand,   7030
He said, "Fellow, you hit me."
"Indeed I did, and I meant to.
But I haven't done you much harm.
As God is my witness, I'm truly
Sorry I had to—but you spoke   7035
Such stupid, insulting words."
"Hah! That won't stop me
From telling you what you deserve.
I don't accept your apology:
You'll lose your hand and your arm   7040
For striking such a blow!"
     As this was going on,
The wounded knight managed
To recover the power of speech,
And said to my lord Gawain,   7045
"Never mind this squire, good sir.
Arguing with such a man
Can only bring you dishonor.
Ignore him, that's my advice:
Just bring me that nag he was riding,   7050
And help this girl you see

Beside me ready her palfrey
For riding, and then, if you please,
Help her mount, for I wish
To stay here no longer. I'll leave,   7055
Riding off, if I possibly
Can, on that nag and seeking
Someone who can give me confession,
For how can I be at ease
Before I've been able to confess   7060
And my soul has received the last rites?"
Gawain immediately fetched
The nag, and brought it to the knight,
Whose eyesight had been fully restored;
He was able, for the very first time,   7065
To see my lord Gawain —
And immediately knew who he was.
Meanwhile, Gawain was assisting
The girl, politely helping her,
As courtesy required he should,   7070
To mount her Norwegian palfrey.
And while he assisted the girl,
The knight took Gawain's horse,
Mounted it, and began to make
Gringolet jump about.   7075
Gawain watched him galloping
Up and down the hill,
Shocked and amused at once,
And finally said, laughing,
"By God, good knight, this   7080
Is really foolish, making
My horse leap like that.
Dismount, and let me take him,

For you're likely to hurt yourself,
Making your wounds reopen."   7085
He answered, "Gawain, be quiet.
You might as well take the nag,
For now you've lost your horse.
I made him jump on purpose,
And now I'll take him for my own."   7090
"Ah! I came here to help you,
And you play me such a dirty trick!
Stealing my horse, like this,
Is treachery; that's what it is!"
"Gawain, with just that same malice,   7095
No matter what it cost me,
I'd rip your heart right out
Of your belly with my own two hands."
"You make me think of a proverb,"
Replied Gawain. "The reward   7100
For doing good deeds is a broken
Neck. All the same,
I'd like to know why you want
Both my heart and my horse.
So far as I know, I've never   7105
In all my life tried to hurt you.
How have I deserved
Such behavior, here, at your hands?
Have I ever seen you before?"
"Oh yes, Gawain, you saw me,   7110
And you covered me with shame.
Don't you remember the man
You forced into eating with dogs,
And kept me there for a month,
And caused me such pain, my hands   7115

Bound behind my back?
That was wild behavior,
As perhaps your shame will show you,
Now." "It's you, then, Gregorias*—
You who raped a girl   7120
For the sheer fun and pleasure of it.
But you ought to know King Arthur's
Country protects its girls
And guarantees their virtue.
The king gives them safe-conduct,   7125
Allowing them freedom of movement.
I can't believe—and I don't!—
That because you were treated badly,
And deserved it, you're harming me,
Because what I did was lawful,   7130
Established by law, and observed
All over Arthur's lands."
"Gawain, how well I remember
What you like to call your 'justice.'
Let it be justice for you   7135
As well. Now it's your turn.
I'm taking your Gringolet:
It's the best revenge I can manage.
You beat that squire. Go steal
His horse: that's the best you can do!"   7140
          And then Gregorias left him,
And the girl who loved Gregorias
Followed him on her palfrey,
Riding very rapidly,
Which made the other girl   7145

* Guinganbresil's brother

Laugh, and she said, maliciously,
"Ah fellow, fellow, what now?
Isn't it time to admit
That the world still holds its share
Of fools? Following you   7150
Is such pleasure! As God is my witness,
You couldn't talk me into turning
Back: I'm so glad to be here!
I regret, however, that the nag
The squire so thoughtfully left you,   7155
And you'll be riding, can't really
Be a donkey. I'd like that, you know,
For then you'd truly be shamed."
Gawain quickly mounted
The stupid, slow-footed nag: 7160
There was nothing better to be had.
It was truly a terrible horse,
With a spindly neck and huge
Head, great drooping ears,
So gap-toothed with age that its sagging   7165
Chops couldn't get closer
Than two whole fingers of touching
Each other—a scrawny, feeble
Beast, with cloudy eyes,
Clawlike hooves, its flanks   7170
Worn down by digging spurs,
A scraggly mane, a bony
Spine. Frayed rope
Was all the bridle and reins
It had; the saddle was bare,   7175
As old as the animal itself,
And the spurs so thin and stretched

They could bear almost no weight.
"Ah, that's the way to go!"
Exulted the wasp-tongued girl.   7180
"How delighted I'll be, now,
To follow wherever you go;
How right it all seems that I cheerfully
Trail along behind you
For a week, or two, or even   7185
Three, or perhaps a month.
Now you're properly equipped,
Mounted on the perfect steed!
Now you've become an appropriate
Guide for leading a girl around!   7190
At last I'll have the pleasure
Of seeing you come to grief.
Why not prod your horse
A bit, spur it on—
Don't be afraid: you've got   7195
A splendid stallion, light
On its feet! Don't worry yourself:
I won't be leaving until
I see you properly shamed.
I'm sure you won't disappoint me."   7200
He answered, "My dear sweet friend,
You can say whatever you like,
Though once a girl has reached
The age of ten she shouldn't
Be guilty of such naughty talk,   7205
But try to exhibit her excellent
Breeding and courteous manners."
"Oh exceedingly unfortunate knight,
Don't try to give me lessons:

Just shut your mouth and ride,   7210
For now you've achieved exactly
The state I was hoping to see."
They rode along until evening,
And both of them held their tongues.
He led the way, and she followed,   7215
Though he found it hard to lead,
Riding the horse he had,
For nothing he did could make it
Gallop. It went on walking
Along; when he tried to use   7220
The spurs, it trotted so hard
That his guts shook; and finally
He simply let it walk,
Since walking was all it could do.
Riding this nag, he crossed through   7225
Barren and lonely forests,
And at last arrived at open
Fields along a deep-flowing
River, so broad a stream
That not even a catapult   7230
Could hurl a stone across,
And no crossbow could fire so far.
On the opposite bank sat a castle,
Beautifully built, exceedingly
Strong, and obviously rich: 7235
I'm obliged to tell you the truth.
Constructed high on a cliff,
The castle was so elaborately,
Richly fortified
That no one living has seen   7240
Its like, a palace built

Entirely of brown marble
And set in native rock.
More than five hundred windows
Were open, filled with ladies   7245
And girls, all of them looking
Down at the meadows and brilliantly
Flowering gardens spread
Before their eyes. Most
Of the girls were dressed in satin,   7250
Though some were wearing tunics
Of many different colors,
And gold-embroidered silk.
      The girls stood in those open
Windows, displaying their shining   7255
Hair and graceful bodies,
For even from the ground one saw them
Well, from their waists to their heads.
And that most malicious creature
In the world, the girl that Gawain   7260
Was leading, went straight to the river,
Stopped, descended from her white-footed
Palfrey, and found a boat
Moored at the bank, locked
To a chain attached to a nearby   7265
Boulder. An oar was lying
In the boat, and on the block
Of stone was the key that opened
The lock. The girl got into
The boat—she and the savage   7270
Heart that beat in her belly—
And her palfrey got in, too,
For he'd done this many times.

"You," she said to Gawain.
"Get in here, hurry up,   7275
You and that miserable horse
Of yours, as skinny as a bird,
And cast off that chain: you're about
To be in plenty of trouble
Unless you quickly cross   7280
This river and get to safety."
"Really?" he said. "And why?"
"You haven't seen what I see?"
She said. "If you had, knight,
I think you'd be moving faster."   7285
Then Gawain quickly turned
His head and, seeing a knight
Riding across the fields,
Fully armed, asked
The girl, "Tell me, if you please,   7290
Just who that might be, riding
Toward us, mounted on my horse,
Stolen away by that traitor
Whose wounds I cured this morning?"
"In the name of Saint Martin,* I'll gladly   7295
Tell you," said the girl. "But let me
Remind you, I'd never give you
So much as a hint, if I thought
My words would do you a bit
Of good. But since I'm sure   7300
The information won't help you,
I won't conceal it. That knight
Is the nephew of your friend Gregorias,

* Model of Christian charity, especially venerated in the city of Troyes

Who's sent him riding after you,
And the reason I tell you this   7305
Is simply because you asked me.
His uncle's ordered him
To chase you down and kill you,
Then bring him your head as a gift.
And now, as I said, get down   7310
Off your horse, unless you're anxious
For death. Hurry and get in here!"
"Girl, I'll never run
From him. I'll wait till he comes."
"I won't even try to stop you,"   7315
Said the girl. "I've nothing more
To say. But what a show
You'll put on, what a display
For all those pretty girls,
Watching from those windows up there!   7320
They've come there just for you,
And you'll give them such a good time!
How happy they're going to be,
Seeing you beaten to the ground!
Ah, you look so much   7325
Like a knight desperate for combat,
No matter what it might cost him!"
"My girl, I've no intention
Of running. I'll go to meet him.
And if I can get back my horse   7330
I'm going to be wonderfully happy."
        Then Gawain quickly turned
The old nag's head toward
The knight, who was galloping at him
Down the riverbank. And Gawain   7335

Let his opponent come
To him, setting himself
In his stirrups so firmly that they broke,
Making the saddle bow bend
To the left, while he leaned   7340
To the right. How else could he hope
To meet the knight, since his nag
Couldn't be moved, no matter
How hard the spurs might dig in?
"Lord!" he said. "Whoever   7345
Wants to distinguish himself
In combat shouldn't be riding
On a nag!" And the knight came dashing
Toward him on a quick-footed, healthy
Horse, and hit Gawain   7350
Such a blow with his lance that it bent
And broke in two, though the point
Remained in Gawain's shield.
But my lord Gawain struck
With his sword, on the upper rim   7355
Of the other's shield, and smashed
Through shield and mail shirt, too,
And toppled him down on the sand.
Gawain reached out, grasped
The reins, and jumped on Gringolet's   7360
Back. And how happy he was!
Nothing he'd ever done
In all his life had filled
His heart so full of joy!
He turned and went back to the girl,   7365
Whose escort he'd been, but couldn't
Find her anywhere in sight:

She and the boat were both gone,
And he felt a certain chagrin,
Losing her in such a way,   7370
Not knowing what might have happened.
     And as he thought of the girl,
He saw a barge approaching,
Poled by a sturdy boatman
Who was clearly coming from the castle.   7375
And when he reached the shore
The boatman called, "Sir,
I bring you greetings from those girls
Up there, who also ask you
To pay me for services rendered.   7380
So pay me now, if you please."
And Gawain replied, "May God
Bless those beautiful girls,
And you along with them, my friend.
You won't be cheated, on my   7385
Account, of anything you're due.
Believe me, I'll do you no wrong.
But what sort of fee are you owed?"
"Sir, you've fought and beaten
A knight, right here on this shore,   7390
Whose horse belongs to me.
If you'd like to treat me fairly
You'll let me have that horse."
Said Gawain, "My friend, that
Would cost me far too much: 7395
I'd be forced to travel on foot."
"Ha, good knight! Those girls
You see up there will take you,
Right away, for a most

Unfaithful man. You've got   7400
To pay me my fee. No one,
So far as I know, has ever
Heard of a combat fought
On this shore without the horse
Of the beaten knight going   7405
To me. At least, if I don't get
The horse, I've got to get
The knight." "Take him, my friend,
And gladly. Keep him, if you like."
"By God, he's not so badly   7410
Hurt," said the boatman. "So I can't.
I think you'd better get him
For me yourself. You're strong
Enough to fetch him, if he starts
Fighting again. If   7415
You're brave enough, go get him
And bring him here to me,
And that will settle your debt."
"My friend, if I dismount
And fetch him, can you be trusted   7420
To watch my horse for me?"
"Yes, indeed," was the answer.
"I'll be his faithful watchman,
And gladly give him back:
Believe me, as long as I live   7425
I'll never do you any wrong.
You have my word, on my honor."
"That's good enough for me,"
Said Gawain. "I take you at your word."
He got down from his horse at once,   7430
As the boatman had asked, and gave

The man his horse's reins.
And then, his sword unsheathed,
My lord Gawain approached
The beaten knight, who wanted 7435
No more fighting, badly
Wounded and bleeding freely.
As Gawain came cautiously toward him
He said, terribly frightened,
"Sir, to tell you the truth, 7440
I'm seriously hurt, and not
Anxious to suffer any more.
I've lost a gallon of blood:
I throw myself on your mercy."
"All right. Get up," said Gawain. 7445
The knight was barely able
To stand. Then Gawain led him
To the boatman, who thanked him for the gift.
Then Gawain asked him if he knew
What might have happened to the girl 7450
He'd brought there with him, and where
She might have vanished. The boatman
Replied, "Sir, don't worry
Yourself about that girl
(Who's not, in fact, a girl 7455
Any more), who's worse than Satan
Himself. Ah, how many
Knights have had their heads
Cut off, right here, because
Of her! Trust me, sir, 7460
Just come and lodge with me,
Tonight, in my very own house.
It won't be to your advantage

To linger long on these shores,
For this is a savage land   7465
Where incredible things can happen."
"My friend, since that's your advice,
I'm much inclined to accept it,
No matter what may come."
    So he did as the boatman suggested,   7470
Stepping on board the boat
And taking his horse with him.
And they crossed to the other side.
The boatman's house was near
The river—so rich and fine   7475
A dwelling, so full of comforts,
That a count could have slept in its rooms.
The boatman led in his guest
And his captive, immensely happy
To have them in his house. My lord   7480
Gawain was served as a knight
Of his fame and courage deserved:
He dined on pigeon and pheasant,
On venison and partridge,
And drank clear unmixed wine,   7485
Both white and red, both new
And aged. The boatman was as pleased
With his prisoner as with his guest.
Once they had eaten, the table
Was removed, and they washed their hands.   7490
Gawain's lodging, that night,
And his host, were all he could want;
The service he was offered, and received,
Was deeply appreciated.
Next day, as soon as the light   7495

Of dawn could be seen, Gawain
Arose early, as he ought to
And as he always did.
And strictly for love of his guest
The boatman arose with him,   7500
And they stood together in a little
Tower, looking out
Its windows. Gawain stared
At the lovely country around them,
Seeing forest and fields   7505
And the castle high on its cliff.
"If it please you, my host," he said,
I'd like to have you tell me
Who is the lord of this land,
And whose is that castle over there."   7510
And then his host replied,
"Sir, I don't know." "You don't?
I find that wonderfully strange,
For you've told me there are soldiers in there,
And you do business with the castle,   7515
And you still don't know its lord!"
"Truly," said the boatman, "I neither
Know nor ever knew."
"Tell me, then, good host,
Who keeps and defends the castle."   7520
"Sir, it's very well guarded,
Five hundred bows and crossbows
Always ready to shoot.
And any invader would find
They'd go on shooting forever   7525
And wouldn't get tired, for they're fired
By extremely ingenious machines.

And I also know this: they're governed
By a queen, a wise and noble
Lady from a royal family.   7530
She came here, with all the gold
And silver treasure she owned,
In order to live in this land,
And built herself the powerful
Castle and noble palace   7535
You see for yourself right there.
And she brought with her a lady
She loves so deeply she calls her
A queen, and says she's her daughter,
And that one has a daughter,   7540
Too, who's never dishonored
Or shamed her family name.
She's said to be the most beautiful,
Best-bred girl in the world.
Art and enchantment both   7545
Protect the great hall of that castle,
And I know enough about it
To tell you the entire story.
The queen brought here a learned
Astronomer priest, who performed   7550
Such incredible feats of magic
In that palace that any knight
Who so much as dared to try
Couldn't get in and couldn't
Stay alive, if he did,   7555
Not for a minute, unless
He'd lived a life free
Of cowardice and devoid of any
Sin, or lying, or greed.

No coward or traitor could survive,   7560
No man of bad faith or deceit.
They'd all be dead on the spot,
And nothing on earth could save them.
There are plenty of young men in that castle,
Gathered from around the world,   7565
Who can handle weapons well,
Perhaps five hundred in all,
Some of them bearded, some not:
A hundred quite without beards,
A hundred who've begun to grow them,   7570
A hundred who shave and shape
Their beards every week,
A hundred whose beards are white
As wool, a hundred all gray.
Many old ladies live there,   7575
Women without a husband
Or lord, wrongly deprived
Of the lands and honors they held
Now that their husbands are dead.
There are orphaned girls, too,   7580
Who live with the two queens
And are treated with great respect.
People like that have come
To this castle, and remained, living
In wonderfully foolish hope   7585
That someday, somehow, a knight
Will come and rescue them all,
Providing husbands for the girls,
Giving the ladies back
Their honors, and making the boys   7590
Knights. But oceans will turn

To ice before any
Such knight will ever appear,
Able to be at once
Wise and generous, quite   7595
Without greed, handsome, brave,
And faithful, unable to do evil.
If such a knight exists,
And comes there, he could rule that castle,
And give the ladies their lands,   7600
And turn war into peace.
The girls would all get married,
And the boys would turn into knights
And quickly, easily lift
Away the magic that binds them."   7605
          My lord Gawain liked
This story; it pleased him immensely.
"Good host," he said, "Let's
Come down from this tower. Bring me,
Please, my horse and my armor: 7610
I can't linger any longer,
I've got to leave." "But where?
Stay, Lord love you, at least
Another day or two."
"Not this time, good host. But blessings   7615
On this house of yours! As God
Is my witness, I need to go.
I want to see those ladies
And the magic ruling that place."
"Oh no, sir! In the name of God,   7620
That's foolish: don't do it. Listen
To me, please, and stay here."
"Good host," said Gawain, "don't take me

For a shiftless, faithless coward!
May God give me up for lost   7625
If I listen to such advice!"
"Sir, I'll hold my tongue:
I can see my words would be wasted.
You want to go, and you'll go,
And although it gives me pain   7630
It seems only right that I guide you
On your way, for no one else
Could help you do what you wish to.
But let me ask for one favor."
"And that, good host? Tell me."   7635
"Promise me, first, you'll grant it."
"I'll do as you wish, good host,
Provided it's nothing shameful."
Then the order was given to lead
His horse from the stable, completely   7640
Equipped for combat, and Gawain
Called for his weapons, and his sword,
And spear, and shield were brought.
He put on his armor, and mounted,
Sat high on his saddle and waited   7645
While the boatman made himself ready
To mount his palfrey, prepared
To lead his guest as he'd promised,
Though the destination was not one
He liked. They reached the bottom   7650
Of the stairs in front of the palace,
Where they found a cripple sitting,
Alone, on a bundle of reeds,
Whose wooden leg was silver
Wound around with gold   7655

And bespangled all over with golden
Rings and precious stones.
Nor was he sitting at rest,
For his hands held a pocket-knife
And were busy polishing an ash-wood   7660
Wand. He said nothing
As they walked right by him, and they
Said not a word to him.
And the boatman, coming close
To my lord Gawain, said, "Sir,   7665
Do you know who this cripple is?"
"His wooden leg isn't wood,
By God," Gawain replied,
"And it's quite incredibly lovely!"
"Oh Lord," said the boatman, "he's rich,   7670
All right, he earns a good living!
If you hadn't come with me
As your guide, let me tell you, you'd hear
A good many things you had
No interest at all in hearing!"   7675
Then on they went, together,
Until they came to the palace;
The entryway was high,
The gates beautiful and rich,
Every nail and every   7680
Hinge made of gold (according
To the story). One gate was ivory,
Carved all down its length;
The other was ebony, equally
Elaborately worked, and both   7685
Were ornamented with gold
And all sorts of costly gems.

The ground was paved in green
And red, violet and blue —
And all these different colors   7690
Extremely beautiful, carefully
Worked, beautifully polished.
And there in the great hall
Was a bed, made without wood,
Fashioned only of gold —   7695
Except for the ropes, which were spun
Entirely of the purest silver.
       I'm not inventing this bed,
From every corner of which
There hung a bell. A great   7700
Coverlet, all of silk,
Had been stretched across it, and in each
Of the bedposts great diamonds
Were set, glittering and gleaming
More brightly, and far more clearly,   7705
Than four burning candles.
It was mounted on four sculpted
Heads, sucking in their cheeks,
And each of the heads sat
On a wheel, that turned so easily   7710
It could be pushed by a single finger
From any part of the room
To another, in any direction.
Truly, no king or count
Has ever had such a bed,   7715
Nor ever will. The palace
Walls were covered with brand-new
Tapestries, and the whole building,
Believe me, was solid as rock,

Constructed of quarried marble,   7720
At the top of which were windows
Of such clear glass that, standing
Inside, one could easily see
Whoever approached the palace
And whoever entered its doors.   7725
Parts of the glass were colored
With such magnificence
That no one could hope to describe them,
And I have no wish to attempt
That task, in any detail.   7730
A hundred of the palace windows
Were open, four hundred were closed.
My lord Gawain was careful
To examine everything, looking
Here and there and every-   7735
Where. And when he was done
He called the boatman to his side
And said, "Good host, I've seen
Nothing, here in this palace,
That could make anyone fear   7740
To walk right in. Tell me,
Please, why you warned me
In such strong terms not
To pay a visit to this place.
I think I'll sit on this bed,   7745
For a bit, and rest myself:
It's the best I've ever seen!"
"Ah, good sir! God keep you
From even going near it!
Merely approaching this bed   7750
Would cause you to die the worst

Death that any knight
Could die." "And what should I do?"
"What? I'll tell you, good sir,
For I have some serious interest   7755
In seeing you stay alive.
Just before you came here—
We were still at my house—I begged you
For a favor, but did not say what
I wanted. Now here's what I wish: 7760
Go back to your own country.
Tell all your friends, and all
The people who live there, that you've seen
A palace so exceedingly rich
That no one can believe its wealth,   7765
Neither you nor anyone else."
"I'd also have to say
That God hates me and I'm covered
With shame. Good host, I believe
You're trying to help me. But how   7770
Can I give up my plan, how
Can I keep myself from sitting
On this bed or making a visit
To those girls I saw, yesterday,
Leaning out of their windows?"   7775
Then his host spoke as harshly
As he could: "Those girls? You'll never
Get to see them! Take yourself
Out of here as fast
As you got yourself in, for you,   7780
My good sir, haven't a chance
In the world of seeing them,
Though they can perfectly well

See you, through their clear glass windows—
Those girls, and ladies, and queens,   7785
So help me God, are watching you
Now, from inside their rooms."
"Indeed," said Gawain. "Well,
At least I'll try the bed,
And if I never see   7790
The girls, I still can't believe
That such a bed would exist
If no one was meant to use it,
Some noble man or highborn
Lady—and so, by my soul,   7795
I'll sit there, no matter what happens!"
Seeing that Gawain couldn't
Be stopped, his host gave up.
Nor could he simply stand there
And watch whatever would happen   7800
To his guest, so he turned to leave,
Saying, "Sir, your death
Will weigh on my heart. No knight
Has ever sat on that bed
Without being killed,   7805
For this is a Magic Bed,
Never meant for sleeping
Or rest, not even for sitting:
No one can use it and live.
Your forfeiting your head   7810
Without a hope of ransom
Or redemption fills me with sorrow!
And since neither my love
Nor my words are strong enough
To save you, my God have mercy   7815

On your soul. My heart won't allow me
To stay here and see you die."
      And then he left the palace,
And Gawain, armed and armored
As he was, his shield hung round   7820
His neck, sat on the bed.
And then, at that very moment,
The bed's silver ropes
Groaned, and the bells rang out,
Echoing all through the palace,   7825
And every window flew open
And wonders began to happen
As the magic started to work,
And arrows and crossbow bolts
Came flying through the windows,   7830
Clattering against Sir Gawain's
Shield, though he saw no archers.
And this was exactly the enchantment,
For no one could ever see
Or understand where arrows   7835
And bolts had come from, nor from
Whose bows they came, though you
Should have no trouble believing
The hail of falling missiles
Created a ghastly racket,   7840
And for no amount of gold
Would Gawain have wanted to be there.
And then the windows reclosed
Themselves, without any human
Help, and Gawain began   7845
To remove the arrows stuck
In his shield, many of which

Had pierced his skin as well;
His wounds bled quite freely.
But before he'd cleaned his shield   7850
Another ordeal occurred:
A peasant came in and banged
His club on a door, and the door
Opened, and a terrible lion,
Strong, and angry, and hungry,   7855
Came leaping into the room
And, roaring wildly, attacked
My lord Gawain, raking
His shield with outstretched claws,
As if it were soft as wax,   7860
And forcing Gawain to his knees.
But the knight leapt right up
And, drawing his sharp-edged sword,
Struck so hard that he cut off
The lion's head and his two   7865
Front paws. And Gawain was happy,
Seeing how one paw hung,
Its claws buried in the wood,
Along the outside length
Of his shield, and the other hung,   7870
Again by its claws, on the inside.
Having killed the lion,
He resumed his seat on the bed—
And his boatman-host, smiling
Broadly, quickly came back   7875
To the palace, and found him quietly
At rest. "Sir," he said,
"I'm sure your troubles are over.
It's safe for you to take off

Your armor: you who have come   7880
And accomplished all these things
Have broken the enchantment forever,
And you'll be served, here
In this place, by young and old
Alike, may God be praised!"   7885
        Then squires crowded around him,
Dressed in beautiful clothes,
And all of them dropped to their knees,
Declaring, "Oh good sweet lord,
You are the one we have yearned for   7890
And endlessly awaited, and we offer
You our service—although
We confess it seems to us
You've taken your time about coming!"
Then some of the squires began   7895
Removing his armor, and others
Went out to his horse and led it
Off to the stable. And as
They were taking off his armor,
A strikingly beautiful, alluring   7900
Girl entered the room,
A golden crown on her head,
Her hair easily as yellow-
Bright as gold, or even
Brighter. Her face was white,   7905
But Nature itself had tinted
Her cheeks the purest red.
Truly, she was perfectly made,
Slender, and lovely, and straight.
And many noble, beautiful   7910
Girls followed her in.

And then a young man entered,
Carrying a bundle of clothes,
A tunic, a coat, and a cloak.
The cloak was lined in ermine,   7915
And in sable, blackberry-dark,
Covered over with cloth
Of a flaming red. My lord
Gawain was struck by the sight
Of these beautiful girls, and couldn't   7920
Keep himself from jumping
To his feet, exclaiming, "Welcome,
Welcome! Girls, you're welcome!"
And the girl who'd entered first
Replied, "Good sir, my lady   7925
The queen sends you her greeting.
She has commanded us all
To take you as our rightful lord
And come and offer our service.
Let me promise you, here   7930
And now, my faithful service,
And these girls who have come here with me
Accept you as their lord, for whose
Arrival they have longed, and waited:
They are overjoyed to see,   7935
At last, the best of all knights!
All that remains is for us
To serve you. My lord, we are ready."
They all fell to their knees,
Bowing their heads before   7940
The man they knew they were meant
To serve and honor. My lord
Gawain immediately asked them

To rise, then once more seated
Himself, delighted to see them,   7945
First because they were lovely,
And then because they'd made him
Their prince and ruler and lord.
He was happier than ever before
In his life, with these honors that God   7950
Had given him. Then the same girl
Came forward: "Before she'll see you,
My lady—lacking neither
In courtesy or good sense—
Sends you this clothing, believing   7955
As she does that you must have gone through
Immense troubles and labors,
Suffered endless hardships.
Put these on, and see
If they fit you as well as they should,   7960
For he who is wise will be careful
Of catching cold, when he's been
So warm and his blood's stirred up.
Which is why my lady the queen
Sends you this ermine robe,   7965
To protect you from becoming chilled,
For just as water will turn
To ice, blood will curdle
And clot, when shivering follows
On warmth." The most courteous man   7970
In the world, Gawain answered,
"May my lady the queen enjoy
God's blessing—He in whom
All goodness inheres—and you, too,
Who speak, and act, and look   7975

So well! The queen is wise,
As well as exceedingly courteous.
She understands exactly
What a knight needs, and should have,
And I thank her kindly for sending   7980
Me these clothes to put on.
Please tell her how grateful I am."
"I will, sir, by God," said the girl,
"And very gladly. And now
We'll leave you. You may dress, and consider,   7985
If you like, the sights of this country,
As seen from these windows. And then,
If you please, climb up that tower
And see the forests and meadows,
The rivers and fields, until   7990
I return to bring you to my lady."
And then the girl left him,
And Gawain put on the beautiful,
Costly clothes he'd been brought,
Fixing them around his shoulders   7995
With a buckle that hung from the neck.
And then he decided to see
What could be seen from the tower.
Walking with his boatman-host,
They climbed a spiral staircase   8000
Attached to the outside of the palace,
And came to the top of the tower,
And saw the landscape around them,
Lovelier than words can describe.
My lord Gawain examined   8005
The rivers and level fields,
The forests filled with animals,

Then turned to his host and said,
"By God, good host, how wonderfully
Pleasant to be here, in a place   8010
Furnished with such excellent hunting
As I see in these forests around us."
"Good sir," the boatman replied,
"You'd better not talk about that,
For I've often heard it said   8015
That whoever God so loves
That He makes him master of this place,
Protector and lord, needs
To understand that he's bound
Never again to go out   8020
Of this castle for any reason
Whatever. Which is why I say
You'd better not talk about hunting,
For this is where you must stay:
You'll never leave here again."   8025
"Be quiet, good host!" said Gawain.
"You'll turn me into a madman
If you go on talking like that!
In the name of God, I couldn't
Stay here a week, not   8030
To mention thousands of weeks,
If I thought I couldn't go out
Whenever I wanted to go."
        Then he walked down from the tower,
And went back into the palace,   8035
Worried and deep in thought.
And when the girl with whom
He'd spoken, before, returned,
She found him seated on the bed,

His face exceedingly grim.   8040
Seeing her come, my lord
Gawain stood up, obviously
Displeased, and greeted the girl
With frigid, formal politeness.
She saw at once how his face   8045
And expression had changed; it was perfectly
Clear from both his look
And his voice that something had made him
Angry, but she did not dare
To ask: "Sir, when you please,   8050
My lady will pay you a visit.
And food is ready, too:
You can eat whenever you like,
Either down here or upstairs."
My lord Gawain replied,   8055
"Girl, I've no interest in eating.
Food won't help my body
If I make the mistake of dining
Before I hear the sort
Of news that makes me happy,   8060
Which I very much need to hear."
Surprised and shocked, the girl
Quickly went back to the queen,
Who called her to her side and asked
How the conversation had gone: 8065
"Granddaughter," said the queen, "what mood
Did you find him in, what state
Of mind, this wonderful lord
Our gracious God has given us?"
"Alas, oh noble queen,   8070
I come to you dying of sorrow:

The only words I was able
To hear from our well-bred, noble
Lord were words of deep
Annoyance and anger. Nor   8075
Can I tell you why, for he
Did not choose to explain and I
Do not know nor dared to ask.
But I surely can tell you that when
I met him the first time, earlier   8080
Today, I found him so easy
And courteous of speech, so nobly
Bred, that I listened in rapture,
Savoring his looks and his bearing.
He seems utterly changed,   8085
As if he wished he were dead,
Disliking whatever he sees."
"Don't worry yourself, granddaughter:
He'll be calm and peaceful again,
As soon as I go to see him.   8090
There can't be any sorrow
So heavy on his heart that I can't
Replace it with pleasure and joy."
　　　　Then the queen prepared for her visit
To Gawain, in the palace great hall,   8095
Taking with her the younger
Queen, who was happy to go,
And leading with them at least
A hundred and fifty girls
And as many pages and squires.   8100
The moment my lord Gawain
Saw her coming, holding
The younger queen's hand, his heart

Told him, without any doubt,
That this was indeed the queen   8105
Of whom he'd heard them speak.
Her long hair, hanging
Below her waist, was white,
Which helped him to guess who she was.
And she wore a white silk dress,   8110
Finely embroidered with close-stitched
Golden thread. Seeing
The lady, Gawain didn't
Delay, but went to greet her.
And she greeted him: "Sir,   8115
I'm your second in command, at this palace.
I grant you primary lordship,
Which you've so well deserved.
Do you come to us from King Arthur's
Household?" "My lady, I do."   8120
"And are you, I should like to know,
One of the knights of the king's
Guard, so famous for their courage?"
"No, my lady." "I believe you.
And do you then, please tell me,   8125
Belong to the knights of the Round
Table, the best in the world?"
"Lady," he answered, "I can't
Presume to call myself
The best, or one of the best,   8130
But I'm not among the worst."
And then she said, "Good sir,
You speak with great courtesy,
Claiming neither the highest
Honors, nor admitting to the lowest.   8135

Now tell me about King Lot:
How many sons does he have?"
"Four, my lady." "And their names?"
"My lady, Gawain is the oldest,
And the second is Agravain   8140
The Proud, famous for his strong
Hands. And the names of the two
Youngest are Gerit and Gueret."
Then the queen spoke once more:
"Sir, as God is my witness,   8145
Those are indeed their names.
I wish God had been pleased
To let them be with us, here!
Now tell me: do you know of a king
Named Urien?" "I do, my lady."   8150
"Has he a son at court?"
"Two sons, my lady, both very
Well known. One's name is Yvain,
Famous for courtesy and breeding.
I count the morning fortunate   8155
When I see him, at the start of the day,
So wonderful are his wisdom and his manners.
The other's name is also
Yvain, but he's not a legitimate
Brother, so he's known as the Bastard,   8160
And he is so skilled at combat
That he beats whoever he fights with.
Both these knights are at court,
Courageous, and wise, and courteous."
"Good sir," she said, "now tell me   8165
How Arthur is, these days?"
"Better than ever—exceedingly

Happy and healthy and strong."
"Ah, that's quite normal, for him!
Arthur is a child, you know.   8170
He'll never change, for better
Or worse, if he lives to a hundred.
But there's one thing more I should like
To ask, if it's not too much:
Tell me, please, how the queen   8175
Is keeping, and whether she's happy."
"Surely, my lady—so very
Courteous and lovely and wise
That God has made no model
For comparison, nor words to describe her.   8180
Since He created the first
Woman from Adam's rib,
No woman has enjoyed such fame,
And so well deserves it, for she teaches
And instructs little children   8185
Like the ripest and wisest sage
And, indeed, my lady the queen
Is everyone's model and teacher,
For she radiates goodness as she goes,
It's born and takes life from her.   8190
No one leaves an audience
With her without good counsel,
For she understands what everyone
Needs, and what she must do
To make them happy. And no one   8195
Ignores what my lady the queen
Advises, but honors her words,
Never leaving her company
Displeased, but with pleasure in their heart."

"Will it be different, with me?"   8200
"Lady, it will be the same,
I think, for before I saw you
I felt indifferent to everything,
Sad and oppressed at heart.
And now I feel as happy   8205
As a man can possibly be."
"Sir," said the white-haired queen,
"By the God who gave me life,
Let your joy be twice as great
And forever keep on increasing;   8210
May you never be without it.
And now that you're happy once more,
Let me remind you that your food
Is ready, if you'd care to dine:
You may eat wherever you please.   8215
Your meal can be served right here
Or, if you'd rather, you're welcome
To dine with me, in my rooms."
"My lady, I've no desire
To eat anywhere but here: 8220
I've been told that no knight
Has ever eaten in this hall."
"No one, sir, who left here
Alive, or remained among
The living for many more minutes."   8225
"With your permission, then,
My lady, I'll eat right here."
"I grant it, sir, most gladly,
And you indeed will be
The first to dine in this hall."   8230
And then the queen left him,

Leaving behind her a hundred
And fifty of her loveliest girls,
Who remained to help him as he ate,
To serve and entertain him   8235
In any way he wanted.
And more than a hundred servants
Were in attendance, some
With white hair, others whose hair
Was graying, and some with none,   8240
Some with no beards or mustaches,
And two who stayed on their knees,
One to cut his meat,
The other to pour his wine.
     My lord Gawain had his boatman-   8245
Host eat beside him,
Nor did they eat in haste,
For the meal lasted even
Longer than the feasts of Christmas:
Blackest night had fallen,   8250
And torch after torch had been burned,
By the time their dinner was done.
Words flowed freely, the whole
Time, and after eating,
And before they slept, they merrily   8255
Danced and sang carols,
Sharing joy in their new
Lord, who was loved by all.
And he, when he went to sleep,
Stretched himself out on the Magic   8260
Bed. And one of the girls
Brought him a pillow, so sleep
Would come more comfortably.

And when he woke, the next day,
He found they'd laid out garments   8265
Of silk and ermine. His boatman-
Host appeared beside
His bed, that morning, to help him
Rise, and wash, and dress.
And Clarissant, beautiful,   8270
Wise, well-spoken, who'd been
The first to greet him, was there
Again. And then she went
To the queen, her grandmother, and was greeted
By a hug and a question: "My dear   8275
Sweet girl, please tell me: Has
Our lord risen from his bed?"
"Oh yes, my lady, long since!"
"And where would I find him, my dear?"
"He went to the tower, but whether   8280
He's come back down I don't know."
"I plan to pay him a visit,
My dear. Pray that God
Will give him nothing but pleasure,
Today." The queen hurried,   8285
Anxious to see him once more,
And found him still in the tower,
Standing at one of the windows
And watching a girl, who was coming
Across a meadow, and with her   8290
Was a knight wearing full armor.
Gawain watched from one window,
And his boatman-host from the next,
And there the queens, walking
Together, hand in hand,   8295

Found them staring intently
Down. "Good morning, my lord!"
Both queens said at once.
"May today be joyous and gay,
By the grace of our Father in Heaven,   8300
Who made His daughter His mother!"
"Lady, may He who sent
His son for Christianity's
Glory give you great joy!
And now, if you wouldn't mind,   8305
Come to this window, please,
And tell me, if you possibly can,
Who might that girl be,
Approaching with a knight whose shield,
I see, is painted in quarters?"   8310
"I'll be very glad to tell you,"
Said the queen, after looking down.
"That's the girl—and may Hell's
Fires burn her!—who led you
Here. Don't think about her: 8315
She's full of evil and malice.
And please ignore, as well,
The knight with whom she's traveling,
For he is surely the most
Courageous knight in the world.   8320
Fighting with him is no game,
For standing right here I've seen
Many fine knights killed
At his hands." "Lady," he said,
"I need to speak to that girl: 8325
May I have your leave, if you please?"
"Sir, God does not wish me

To permit you to hurt yourself.
Let that wicked girl
Attend to her own affairs.   8330
God does not want you to leave
This palace for such foolish business.
Nor should you go through these gates
Intending your own harm."
"Ah, my noble queen!   8335
Your words are deeply troubling.
I'll feel myself most unfortunate,
If I can't go out of this castle.
Surely, God does not wish me
To be held captive for so long."   8340
"Oh, lady!" cried the boatman.
"Let him do as he wishes.
If you hold him here against
His will, he may die of sorrow."
"Then I will allow him out,"   8345
Said the queen, "but on this condition:
If God preserves him alive,
He'll return here tonight."
"My lady, don't worry," he said.
"I'll surely return, if I can.   8350
But there's one thing more I need
To ask you, please: don't ask me
My name for another eight days.
Wait, if you possibly can."
"If that's what you want, I'll agree,"   8355
Said the queen, "though it won't be easy.
I've no desire to displease you.
Had you not forbidden the question,
My lord, requesting your name

Would otherwise have been   8360
The very first thing I did."
Then down from the tower he went,
And servants came running to bring him
His weapons, and put on his armor,
And they led out his horse and, completely   8365
Equipped for battle, he mounted.
He rode straight to the gate,
Along with his boatman-host,
And both went on board a boat,
And were rowed so quickly across   8370
That soon they reached the opposite
Bank, and Gawain disembarked.
And the unknown knight said
To the merciless, malicious girl,
"My dear, tell me: do you know   8375
This knight I see over there,
Riding out against us?"
"Not who he is," she said,
"Except that, yesterday,
He was the one who led me   8380
Here." "As God is my guide,"
He said, "that's the one
I want. I was very worried
He might have gotten away.
No knight born of a mortal   8385
Mother can cross the Galloway
Border, if I see him riding
Along and confront him, and none
Can boast they ever came back,
Once they reached this country.   8390
They're taken captive and held,

If God lets me see them."
With that, and without a challenge
Or warning, the knight spurred
His horse and braced his shield,   8395
And Gawain galloped to meet him,
Striking so hard with his spear
That he wounded his arm and his side,
But not badly enough to kill him,
For the mail shirt held, and only   8400
The point of the lance pierced through
And went two fingers deep
Into his body, and he fell
To the ground. He was able to stand,
And did, but both his arm   8405
And his side were bleeding freely,
And the sight gave him no pleasure.
He drew his sword, all the same,
But soon discovered he was far
Too weak to keep on fighting,   8410
And was forced to ask for mercy,
Which Gawain granted, after asking
For his formal surrender, and the waiting
Boatman received the prisoner.
And then the malicious girl   8415
Came down from her palfrey, and Gawain
Approached, and gave her a courteous
Greeting: "Remount, my dear,
For I'm not about to leave you.
I intend to take you with me   8420
To the other bank, where I'm staying."
"Hah!" she said. "Now
You're so fierce and brave, knight!

You would have had a different
Combat on your hands, if my lover   8425
Had not been afflicted by old
Wounds. You wouldn't be so full
Of good humor, or so free with your boasts,
And your mouth would be stuffed by checkmate!
Just tell me the simple truth: 8430
Can you really think you're better
Than him, because you beat him?
You know quite well how often
The weaker beats the stronger.
But come away from the river   8435
For a moment, and ride over
To that tree over there, and just
Do a little something
For me that my lover would have done,
Except that you've got him in your boat,   8440
And if you can do it I'll tell
The world you're better than he is
And I'll stop treating you as I have."
"A simple request like that,"
He said, "shouldn't be too hard   8445
To fulfill. Gladly, my girl."
And she answered, "May God keep me
From having to see you come back!"
And so he went with her,
She in the lead, and he   8450
Behind, and the girls and ladies
Of the palace pulled out their hair,
And ripped and tore at their clothes,
Crying, "Alas, alas!
How can we live, seeing   8455

The knight who should be our lord
Following her, who means
To bring him hurt and shame?
That evil girl, so full
Of malice, is conducting him   8460
To a place no knight can return from!
Ah, how our hearts are hurting,
Though we'd thought ourselves so happy,
God having sent us this knight
So wise and good, lacking   8465
Neither in strength nor in virtue,
Deficient in nothing we needed."
          And thus they expressed the sorrow
They felt, seeing their lord
Follow the wicked girl.   8470
They both arrived under
The tree, and then my lord
Gawain said to her, "Girl,
Tell me, please, if now
I've done what you wanted me to do.   8475
If there's anything else you want
I'll gladly do it, if I can,
Rather than disappoint you."
And then the girl said,
"Do you see that deep ford,   8480
With the steep banks on each side?
And the flowers over there,
In those trees and in those meadows?
My lover would take me down there
Whenever I wanted, so I   8485
Could pick them." "And how could he get there?
I can't even see the ford!

The river runs too high,
And the ford is surely too deep.
How could you possibly reach it?"   8490
"You wouldn't dare, of course,"
Said the girl. "I already knew that.
I never thought you'd have
The courage to make the attempt,
Much less to succeed. That's known   8495
As the Perilous Ford, and no
Merely ordinary knight
Can hope to get across it."
Quickly, my lord Gawain
Rode to the river bank,   8500
And saw the depth of the water
Racing high against it.
But he saw, too, that the river
Was narrow, and remembered that his horse
Had jumped over many wider   8505
Ditches; he also recalled
Hearing it said, here
And there and often, that whoever
Leapt the Perilous Ford
And crossed so deep a stream   8510
Would win the greatest honor
In the world. He rode off
To the side and came galloping back
For the jump, but made the mistake
Of leaping a little too soon   8515
And landed in the middle of the ford,
But his horse swam until
It found the ground with all
Four feet, and set itself firmly,

And jumped again, and this time   8520
Landed up on the high
Bank, where it stood immobile,
Having crossed the river, indeed,
But exhausted and unable to move.
My lord Gawain, aware   8525
Of the horse's fatigue, knew
That something had to be done.
Quickly dismounting, he unbuckled
The saddle straps, removed
The saddle, then laid it down   8530
To dry. Removing the saddle-
Cloth as well, he rubbed
The horse's back and sides
And legs, until it was dry.
Then he put the saddle back   8535
And mounted, riding slowly
Along until he saw
A solitary knight
Hunting with a hawk. Three bird dogs
Lay in the meadow beside him.   8540
This was so handsome a knight
That words could never describe him.
As my lord Gawain approached,
He greeted the hunter, saying,
"Good sir, may God, who made you   8545
The loveliest creature in the world,
Give you good hunting today."
And the other knight replied,
"But it's you who are handsome, and good!
But tell me, if you please, why   8550
You've left that wicked girl

Alone back there. She had
An escort: what happened to him?"
"Indeed," said Gawain. "A knight
With a shield painted in quarters   8555
Was with her, when I met them." "And what
Did you do?" "We fought, and I beat him."
"And what's become of that knight?"
"I gave him to my boatman, who's told me
My prisoners belong to him."   8560
"He's told you the truth, good sir.
I once was that girl's lover,
But not because she ever
Really loved me, or ever
Acknowledged me as her lover,   8565
Or let me so much as kiss her,
Believe me, unless I used force.
I never came close to having
What my heart longed for, from her:
But like it or not, I loved her.   8570
I took her away from another
Knight. I killed him and put
Myself to the trouble of serving
Her. It did me no good:
She left me as soon as she could,   8575
And went with a new lover,
The one you took her away from.
And he's no knight to fool with,
By God, but strong and brave —
And yet, he never dared   8580
Come riding anywhere
He thought he might meet me.
But you, just now, have done

Something no one has ever
Attempted, and earned for yourself,   8585
With great courage and ability,
The highest reward of fame
And honor the world can offer.
Jumping across the Perilous
Ford was a feat of immense   8590
Virtue—and let me say
Again, never before done."
"Sir," said Gawain, "then the girl
Told me a lie, saying—
And I thought she was speaking the truth—   8595
That her lover crossed it every
Day, for love of her."
"The liar! Is that what she said?
She ought to be drowned in that ford
For telling you such nonsense: 8600
She's full of the devil, all right.
She certainly hates you, that's clear,
And hoped it was you who would drown
Down in that deep and treacherous
Water—may God confound her!   8605
Good sir, now give me your word,
We two will make a pact:
Whatever you feel like asking
I'll be obliged to answer,
For better or for worse,   8610
If you ask me something I know.
And you'll do the same for me,
And never tell me any lies,
No matter what I ask you:
If you know the truth, you'll tell me."   8615

Both of them gave their word,
And the first to ask his questions
Was my lord Gawain. "Sir,
He said, "I'd like to know
The name of that city I see   8620
Over there, and who is its lord?"
"My friend," was the answer, "I'll tell you
The whole truth. That city
You see belongs to me;
I hold it free and clear.   8625
My only debts are to God.
And its name is Orquelain."
"And yours?" "I'm Grinomalant."
"Sir, I've certainly heard
Of you, and your courage and valor,   8630
And the size of the lands you hold.
But what's the name of that girl
Of whom no one speaks well,
However far and wide
One goes, as you say yourself?"   8635
"Oh, I can testify
That the further away from her,
The better! She's haughty and evil.
Which is why her name is the Proud
Beauty of Logres. She was born there,   8640
But taken away as a child."
"And her lover's name, who was led
Away, like it or not,
A captive in my boatman's prison?"
"As I've told you, my friend, this   8645
Is a truly remarkable man,
And his name is the Haughty Knight

Of the Rock in the Narrow Road,
Who guards the gate to Galloway."
"And what is the name of that splendid,   8650
Wonderfully beautiful castle
On the other bank, where I ate
And drank last night, and came from
This morning?" And Grinomalant
Turned away, as if   8655
In sorrow, and started to leave.
But Gawain called him back:
"Sir, speak to me, please!
Remember the pledge we made!"
And Grinomalant stopped, turned   8660
His head to the side, and said,
"May the very moment I saw you
And made you the promise you speak of
Be cursed, and damned in shame!
Leave me: I free you from your promise,   8665
And you release me from mine,
For I'd meant to ask you the news
From that castle on the other bank,
But you seem to know as much
About it as you know of the moon!"   8670
"Sir," said Gawain, "I spent
The night there, I slept in the Magic
Bed—which wasn't like
Any bed I know of!"
Grinomalant said, "Sir,   8675
This is astonishing news.
You make me very happy,
Telling these lies I've just heard;
I listen to you as I listen

To other fine storytellers!   8680
You're clearly a minstrel; I see that.
Alas, I took you for a knight,
Someone who might have done
Courageous deeds down there.
But try to tell me the truth: 8685
Have you ever been a knight? Have you
Been witness to things worth describing?"
My lord Gawain replied,
"Sir, when I sat on that bed
The palace fairly exploded—   8690
Don't think I'm telling you lies!—
The very bed ropes were moaning,
And bells were ringing like mad,
Hanging as they were from that bed.
Then all the windows, which were closed,   8695
Suddenly opened by themselves,
And steel-tipped arrows and crossbow
Bolts struck my shield,
Which also received the claws
Of a huge lion, with a mane,   8700
Who'd been lying in wait for a very
Long time, chained in a room.
That lion was directed at me
By a peasant, who freed him from his chains.
The lion came leaping at me,   8705
And struck at my shield with his paws,
But his sharp claws stuck
In the wood, he couldn't retract them.
If you think I'm telling you tales,
Look: his claws are hanging   8710
Right here! God be thanked,

I cut off his head, and his paws.
Here's the proof: can you see it?"
Grinomalant dismounted
And quickly fell to his knees,   8715
His head bowed, his hands
Bent in supplication,
Begging pardon for his folly.
"I forgive you. Of course!" said Gawain.
"Remount, if you please." And he did,   8720
Though very ashamed of himself:
"Sir, as God is my Saviour,
I couldn't believe that any
Knight from far or near
Could ever have earned the enormous   8725
Honor you've won! Tell me,
Please: did you happen to see
The white-haired queen, and did
You ask her who she was
And where she came from?" "I saw her,   8730
And we spoke, but I never thought
To ask." "I'll tell you, then,"
Said Grinomalant. "That white-haired
Queen is King Arthur's mother."
"By the faith I owe to God,"   8735
Said Gawain, "Arthur's mother
Died a great many years
Ago—at least sixty,
I think, but perhaps even more."
"But she is truly his mother.   8740
When Uther Pendragon, his father,
Was laid in the earth, Queen
Ygerne came to this country,

Bringing with her all
Her treasure, and then she built   8745
A castle high on that rock,
And that rich and beautiful palace
You've seen for yourself. You've also
Seen, I know you have,
That other great lady, that other   8750
Queen, the beautiful woman
Who once was the wife of King Lot
And mother—I curse the name!—
Of Gawain." "Gawain, my dear sir,
Is someone I know quite well,   8755
And he has not had his mother
For twenty years or more."
"But all the same, it's true.
She came here after her mother,
Pregnant with a healthy baby—   8760
The noble, beautiful girl
I love, and Gawain's sister.
Sir, I tell you no lies:
May God give Gawain endless
Shame! Not even the Lord   8765
Himself could save that man,
If I had him here in front
Of me, standing where you are:
I'd cut off his head—like that!
His sister couldn't help him: 8770
I hate him so much I'd tear
The heart right out of his belly."
"Clearly," said Gawain, "you don't
Love the way I do!
If I loved a girl, or a lady,   8775

For the sake of her love I'd love
Her family, too, and serve them."
"You're right; I can't disagree.
But when I think of Gawain
I remember his father killing   8780
Mine, and how can I wish him
Well? And Gawain himself
Killed one of my cousins,
A brave and valiant knight.
I've never yet had a chance   8785
To work the revenge I long for.
But you can do me a service:
The next time you go to that castle,
Carry this ring to my love,
On my behalf. And when   8790
You put it in her hands, I wish
You'd tell her my love is true,
And I trust her love so much
I believe she'd rather see
Her brother Gawain die   8795
Horribly than I have a scratch
On the littlest toe of my foot.
Give my love my greetings
As you give her, from me, this ring,
For I am her true belovèd."   8800
Gawain put the ring
On the smallest finger of his hand,
And said, "Sir, I must tell you
Your belovèd must be courteous and wise,
Born of the noblest blood,   8805
And beautiful, charming, and gracious,
If she agrees with all

You've told me, in every detail."
"Sir," was the answer, "you'll do me
A great favor, I assure you,   8810
If you bring that ring to my dear
Belovèd, for whom my love
Is immense, as a present from me.
And in return for that favor
I'll tell you, exactly as you asked,   8815
The name of that castle. It's called
(You seem not to have heard this)
The Rock of Champguin, and its walls
Are lined with beautiful red
And scarlet cloth, in which   8820
They do much business, buying
And selling.
                 "I've answered whatever
You've asked, without any lies;
You've given me useful news.
Is there anything else you wish?"   8825
"Only permission to leave you."
"Before I let you go,
Good sir, tell me your name,
If you've no objection." "None,"
Said my lord Gawain. "I've never   8830
Considered my name a secret.
I am the man you hate
So much, I am Gawain."
"You are Gawain?" "Indeed
I am, King Arthur's nephew."   8835
"By God, you're either incredibly
Brave, or insanely foolish,
To tell me your name, in the face of

My hatred. How I regret
Not having my helmet laced 8840
And my shield hung from my neck,
For had I my weapons and armor,
As you do, rest assured
I'd quickly cut off your head:
I'd never spare you, Gawain! 8845
If you're brave enough to wait
Right here, while I fetch my armor,
I'll hurry back, and we'll fight.
I'll bring three or four men
To witness our combat. Or, 8850
If you wish, we can do it differently,
Waiting exactly a week
And then returning here
To this place, armored and ready,
And you can have the king 8855
And queen to watch, and whoever
You like, and I'll bring my people
From all around the country,
And then the battle between us
Won't be a private affair 8860
But in front of all who wish
To watch it, as public as it ought
To be, with two such knights
As our reputations make us:
Other knights, and ladies, 8865
Should enjoy the right to behold us.
And then, when one of us loses,
The whole world will know it,
And the winner will earn honor
Infinitely greater, when the news 8870

Is much more widely known."
"Sir," said my lord Gawain,
"I'll gladly oblige you, and require
A good deal less, if a battle
Can be readily arranged, and you want one.   8875
If, however, amends
Can be made for whatever wrong
I may have done you, I suspect
Our mutual friends can find
A solution." "I see no reasonable   8880
Way," was the answer, "if you aren't
Willing, or able, to fight me.
I've given you two clear choices:
Pick whichever you want.
If you dare, just wait right here,   8885
And I'll go and get my armor.
Or you can tell your friends
To be here in exactly a week.
I've heard King Arthur's court
Is always at Orcanie,   8890
For Pentecost, and that's
A ride of at most two days.
Your messenger should find
The king and his people quite ready.
Send him: as everyone knows,   8895
Time is worth more than money."
"God save me," said Gawain, "surely
The court will be there, as you say.
Your information's correct.
I hereby give you my word   8900
I'll send someone tomorrow,
Before I close my eyes."

"And now, Gawain, I'd like
To show you the best bridge
In the world. This river's too deep   8905
And dangerous for anyone to cross it
Alive, and it can't be jumped."
My lord Gawain replied
He had no interest in bridges
Or fords, whatever they were like: 8910
"That wicked girl, who's waiting
For me to return, as I promised
To do, will tell the world
I'm a coward, unless I come back."
A flick of his spurs, and his horse   8915
Leaped straight across the river,
As if it were only a ditch.
Seeing him safely across,
The girl, whose tongue had soundly
Whipped him back and forth,   8920
Dismounted, tied her palfrey
To a tree, and came walking toward him,
Looking completely changed.
Her greeting was modest and polite,
And she said, at once, that she meant   8925
To ask forgiveness for her wrongs,
And for all the pain she'd caused him.
"Good sir," she said, "give me
The chance to explain just why
I've shown such arrogance   8930
To all the knights who've met me.
I hope you'll let me tell you.
The knight you spoke to, on the other
Bank (may God destroy him!),

Was wasting his love on me: 8935
He loved me, but I hated him!
What pain and suffering he caused me,
Killing—I'm telling the truth—
The man I truly loved!
He thought he could win my heart   8940
By showering me with honor.
He never succeeded; he couldn't.
I fled him, the very first moment
I could, and went, instead,
With the knight from whom you took me   8945
Today—who's worth about
As much to me as a clove
Of garlic! After my original
Lover was taken by death,
Grief drove me insane,   8950
And I spoke with such wild pride,
Such wicked, half-crazed folly,
That it made no difference to me
Who might suffer for my words.
Indeed, I did it all   8955
Deliberately, hoping
I'd find someone so easily
Angered I'd drive him to distraction
And he'd cut me to little pieces:
For a long, long time I've wanted   8960
To be dead. Now deal with me
However justice may require,
So girls, hearing my story,
Won't shame and slander knights."
"My dear," he said, "who   8965
Am I to bring you to justice?

Our Lord in Heaven won't like it,
If punishment comes from me.
Hurry, and mount your horse,
And we'll ride to the castle I came from.   8970
My boatman's waiting, there
On the bank, to take us across."
"My lord, I'll do whatever
You ask," replied the girl.
And then she mounted her little   8975
Palfrey, with its flowing mane,
And they rode to where the boatman
Was waiting, and without any trouble
Or fuss he took them across.
And all the ladies and girls   8980
Who'd so much mourned his going
Saw him coming back.
And so did the pages and squires,
Who'd been half-mad with grief.
All were happier, now,   8985
Than they'd ever been in their lives.
The queen was seated in front
Of the palace, awaiting their coming,
Surrounded by her girls, singing
And dancing all together,   8990
In order to express their pleasure—
Singing and dancing carols,
Moved by their joy and relief.
He came, and dismounted in their midst.
And the ladies and girls, joined   8995
By the two queens, hugged him,
And told him how happy they were,
And celebrated as they took off

His armor, piece by piece.
And the girl he'd brought there with him   9000
Was also received with great joy,
All of them wanting to serve her,
But on his behalf, not hers.
They paraded them into the palace,
Where everyone inside was seated   9005
And waiting, and Gawain took
His sister to sit beside him
On the Magic Bed, and said,
Carefully lowering his voice,
"My dear, I bring you a little   9010
Ring from the land on the other
Bank, a lovely green emerald.
A knight sent it, for love
Of you, and sends you his greetings,
And declares you his dearly belovèd."   9015
"How nice, good sir," she said,
"But I cannot love him very much,
Knowing him only at a distance,
Nor has he ever seen me
Except from across the river.   9020
But I know he's long since offered
His love (for which I thank him),
And even if he hasn't come here
He's sent me so many words
Of love that I've promised to love him,   9025
And that's the whole story.
Nothing else has happened."
"Ah, my dear! He's boasted
You already love him so much
You'd rather see my lord   9030

Gawain, your brother, die
Than have him hurt his toe!"
"Oh sir, how can he say
Such wild and foolish things!
Lord, I never thought   9035
He could be so badly bred.
He's thrown prudence to the winds,
Sending me such a message.
Heavens! My brother doesn't
Even know I'm alive.   9040
He's never seen me. And this
Is all wrong: upon my soul,
I wish for no such thing!"
      And as they sat there, talking,
The ladies watched them closely,   9045
And the old queen, seated
Beside her daughter, said,
"Dear daughter, how do you like
That gentleman there, sitting
Next to your lovely daughter?   9050
They've talked for quite some time —
Who knows of what? — but it's not
Something to worry about:
Clearly, his noble heart
Finds itself attracted   9055
To the best, most beautiful, wisest
Girl in this palace — and rightly!
May it please God she pleases
Him as Aeneas was pleased
By Lavinia, and they marry, these two!"   9060
"Ah lady," the other queen said,
"May God so bend his heart,

For they seem like brother and sister,
And if they loved each other
They'd truly be joined into one!"   9065
She meant, of course, that the two
Should be joined as man and wife,
Not recognizing her son.
They were like brother and sister,
And that was how they would love,   9070
Once the girl had learned
She was his sister and he
Her brother. Her mother would be happy,
But not as she'd thought she would.

      Gawain had said what he needed   9075
To say to his beautiful sister,
So he rose and called to his side
A servant he'd seen, standing
To his right, who struck him as modest
But brave, anxious to please,   9080
And the wisest, most sensible page
Of all the young men in that hall.
And then he went to a room
Off the hall, and the youngster went with him.
When the door was closed, and they   9085
Were alone, he said, "Young man,
I think you're well-trained and clever.
I'm going to tell you something—
But you need to keep it a secret,
In your own best self-interest.   9090
I propose to send you somewhere
Where your message will be greeted with joy."
"Sir, I'd let them pull
The tongue right out of my mouth

Before I let myself speak   9095
A single, solitary word
You wanted to hide away."
"My friend," said Gawain, "you'll go
Straight to King Arthur's court.
I am Gawain, his nephew.   9100
The trip will neither be long
Nor hard, but only to Orcanie,
Where the king has set up his court
To keep the Pentecost feast.
Whatever expenses you have   9105
On the way will be mine to pay.
When you stand in front of the king,
Remember, you'll find him displeased,
But as soon as you greet him in Gawain's
Name, he'll be happy once more.   9110
Indeed, no one who hears
The news you'll bring will be sad!
Tell the king that, by
The faith between lord and man,
On the fiftth day of the feast   9115
He's to come (on whatever pretext
He likes) to the foot of this tower
And set up his camp, and he's
To have with him such men
And women of high and middle   9120
Rank as may be at his court,
For I'm to fight in combat
Against a knight who thinks
Little of the king or of me.
His name is Grinomalant,   9125
And he hates me with a deadly passion.

And tell the queen to come,
Too, by the great faith
We've given one another,
She my lady, and I   9130
Her friend, and let her spread
The news as widely as she can,
And lead here, for love of me,
As many of the ladies and girls
At her husband's court who can join her.   9135
But one thing still worries me:
Have you a horse speedy
Enough to get you there
In time?" The young man replied
That he had the use of excellent   9140
Horses, fast and strong.
"Good," said Gawain. "I'm glad
To hear it." Then the youngster led him
To the stables, and brought out, for Gawain
To see, a number of large,   9145
Well-rested horses, one
Of whom was completely ready
To travel wherever was wanted,
Not only newly shod
But saddled and bridled as well.   9150
"By God," said my lord Gawain,
"You come well-equipped, youngster!
Now go straight to our lord
The king, go and return,
And stick to the narrow path!"   9155
          The messenger went on his way,
Escorted as far as the river
By my lord Gawain, who ordered

The boatman to ferry him
Across—a task that presented 9160
No obstacles at all,
For the boatman had many men
At the oars. The youngster hurried
On toward Orcanie,
Well aware that knowledge 9165
Of roads can lead a man
Wherever he wants in the world.
And my lord Gawain returned
To his palace, remaining there
In great joy and delight. 9170
Everyone celebrated,
And the queen ordered five hundred
Baths and sweat-rooms to be heated,
So all the young men would be able
To bathe and wash as they liked. 9175
Brand-new clothes had been made,
So when they emerged from their baths
They were well and properly dressed.
The fabrics were all good silk;
The fur was ermine. And then 9180
The young men stayed in church
All morning, standing as they prayed,
Never kneeling once.
And later that morning, with his own
Hands, my lord Gawain 9185
Put a spur on each one's right foot,
Buckled on a sword, and dubbed each one
A knight. And he had a company
Of half a thousand new knights!
      Meanwhile, his messenger rode 9190

So fast that he'd reached the city
Of Orcanie, where King Arthur
Held court in royal style.
Cripples and beggars, watching
As he galloped by, exclaimed,   9195
"There's someone who's truly
In a hurry! He must be bringing
News from some far-off country!
But whatever he tells the king,
He'll find Arthur all out   9200
Of sorts, silent and angry.
But who will there be to give
The king the counsel he'll need,
Once he's heard this message?"
"Tell me," said another. "Are we   9205
Supposed to worry how the king
Searches for wisdom? We're all
Lost and broken, now
That we've been deprived of the man
Who, acting for the love of God,   9210
Kept us alive with alms
And gifts and all manner of charity."
All over the city, the poor
And needy, who deeply loved
Gawain, regretted his absence.   9215
        The messenger kept to the road
And finally came to the palace
Where he knew he could find the king,
With a hundred counts around him,
And a hundred dukes and kings.   9220
        Arthur was pensive and sad.
Seeing himself with so many

Great ones, but without Gawain,
He fainted with distress, and everyone
Rushed to his side, all   9225
Wanting to be the very
First to assist him. My lady
Lorre,* seated in the gallery,
Saw and heard the commotion
Down in the hall, and came there,   9230
Hurriedly, just in time
To find the queen arriving,
Distraught like everyone else,
And seeing my lady Lorre
Guinevere asked if she   9235

     EXPLYCYT PERCEVAX LE VIEL
     ["Here ends the old *Perceval*"] **

---

* In thirteenth-century tales, Lorre is a fairy; in one such tale, she is
Gawain's lover
** Added by an unknown hand, to separate the poem Chrétien did not
finish from its continuation

Afterword

Joseph J. Duggan

Perceval: The Story of the Grail, a masterwork of world literature, was written under the patronage of Philip, count of Flanders and Alsace. This powerful noble Philip was the seneschal of France in 1180, during the reign of King Philip II; his niece, Isabelle of Hainaut, was married to the king, whom Philip of Flanders knighted in June of that year.

Philip of Flanders participated in the Third Crusade, leaving France in September 1190 and dying at Acre in June the following year. The date of Chrétien de Troyes's death is unknown, but he left *Perceval* unfinished, and one of the poets who wrote a continuation, Gerbert de Montreuil, says that Chrétien died before completing this last of his five surviving romances. Some believe that Chrétien must have accompanied Philip on the crusade and that he died in the Holy Land, but others place the composition of *Perceval* almost a decade earlier, in the period of good relations between Champagne and Flanders that began in June 1180. This might explain Chrétien's reference to Philip as the most worthy man in the Holy Roman Empire, since in the period after 1181 Philip took steps to improve his relationship with the emperor, from whom he held several fiefs. Fol-

lowing the death of Philip's wife in March 1182, he began at-
tempts to marry Marie de Champagne, who had been a widow
since Count Henry the Liberal's death the previous year and
was regent of the county of Champagne. Marie was the king's
half-sister and Chrétien's patron for his romance *Lancelot: The
Knight of the Cart.* But Philip of Flanders turned away from this
course of action in the fall of 1183. Anthime Fourrier places the
composition of *Perceval* in this period, between May 1182 and
the autumn of the following year. In this case, Chrétien's death
would not have been connected with the crusade.

Chrétien writes that Philip of Flanders gave him a book con-
cerning the Grail (l. 66). What would this book have contained?
It is likely that we will never know beyond what Chrétien tells
us at various points in the romance, namely that the book was
the source of his knowledge that Perceval kissed Blanchefleur
seven times, that the Hideous Damsel was indeed ugly, and
that Perceval forgot God. The consensus is, however, that the
Grail mystery draws upon Celtic myth, and the source book was
perhaps a link in that chain of transmission.

The objects Perceval encounters during his visit to the Grail
castle recall the talismans of the Tuatha Dé Danaan, the "people
of the goddess Danu," divine figures central to Irish myth. The
talismans are the spear of the god Lug that made its holder un-
conquerable, the cauldron of the Dagda (the "good god") from
which no company went unsatisfied, and the sword of the god
Nodens that pursued the enemy relentlessly once it was drawn.
These three may be the sources respectively of the lance and
Grail that are carried in procession in the Rich Fisher King's
castle and the sword that the king presents to Perceval. That

the Grail, like the Dagda's cauldron, is a vessel of plenty is sug-
gested by its description as a dish in which one might serve a
fish, by the fact that it is carried through the hall at each course
of the king's elaborate feast, and by its being used to carry a
single host that keeps the Fisher King's father, the Grail King,
alive. Another vessel of plenty, this one attested in Welsh lore,
is the platter of Rhydderch, which supplies whatever food one
wishes. In later Grail romances the Grail typically provides food
in abundance, according to the desires of the person who is eating. The fourth talisman of the Tuatha Dé Danaan, the stone of
Fál that cries out under the true ruler, does not have its counterpart in the Grail castle, but since both the Fisher King and the
Grail King are Perceval's kin, it may be that a magic device such
as the stone would have appeared later to determine Perceval's
fitness to inherit the Fisher's kingdom, had Chrétien been able
to complete the romance.

Other parallels to elements in *Perceval* appear in Celtic tradition. The god Nodens is pictured among fish and tridents and
is thus a fisher king. The god Bran bears the epithet "the man
with holes in his thighs," which is thought to signify that he has
been castrated, as is the case with the wounds of both the Fisher
King and Perceval's father. A story pattern found in Irish sagas,
the boyhood deeds of the hero, particularly as exemplified in
The Boyhood Deeds of Finn, contains striking parallels to the
plot of *Perceval*. Finn is brought up by his widowed mother in
obscurity in a forest, travels to the court of the king of Bantry,
takes up with a lover, encounters a woman whose son has been
killed by a warrior whom he pursues and defeats, meets his
uncle in the wilderness, overhears between two fairy mounds
the voices of fairies exchanging questions and answers, sees a
cooked pig being carried out of one of the fairy mounds on a
kneading-trough, and kills a warrior who used to slay anyone

attempting to court his female companion. What Finn overhears includes the question "Is there anything to be brought from us to you?" and the reply "If something is brought to us, something will be brought to you in return for it." The saga contains many elements that bear no resemblance to the plot of the French romance, but like *Perceval,* it recounts the boyhood, coming of age, and training of a hero. *The Boyhood Deeds of Finn* is unlikely to have been the direct source for the plot of *Perceval,* but Chrétien may have had access to some Breton analogue of the Irish tale that is no longer extant.

But whatever the contents of Philip's book, Chrétien's romance, in addition to conveying the mystery of the Grail, is also the story of a boy's progression from the naive state of a child brought up in rural seclusion and imposed ignorance of chivalric institutions to the status of one of the most respected knights of Arthur's court. In this trajectory Perceval has two teachers, his mother, who instructs him on respectful relations with both women and men and on the central elements of the Christian religion, and Gornemant of Goort, whose advice concerns knightly skills and duties and includes an admonition not to speak too much. During the course of the romance, Perceval gains in maturity and thoughtfulness until he is able to reject the choice made at Arthur's court by the other knights to seek worldly adventures. Instead, Perceval decides to devote himself to a search for the answers to the questions he should have asked in the Grail castle.

The bleeding lance is never explained in the romance as we have it from Chrétien. The answer to the second of the two questions that Perceval's cousin identifies is that the Grail was being carried to the Grail King, who had been an invalid for fifteen years and was being sustained by a single communion wafer. Had Perceval asked the question, the Grail King would have been cured, regaining the use of all his limbs, and would have held the land again. The reason for Perceval's failure to ask the questions is revealed, however: in the course of leaving home, he did not turn back to tend to his mother when he saw her fall, and she died of grief at his departure. That this is a sin of which he had no knowledge, according to Perceval's hermit uncle, raises theological questions, since sin implies awareness of culpability for one's acts. Perceval's failure has, then, causes on two planes, the level of human motivation that is explained by his desire to follow Gornemant's counsel, and a spiritual dimension in which the responsibility of the son for his mother dominates.

The relationship between son and mother is only one of the many elements in *Perceval* that involve kinship ties. The romance is, in fact, permeated by the theme of lineage. Virtually all the characters for whom Chrétien inspires sympathy in the reader belong to two royal families, the Grail King's and King Arthur's. Perceval's father has died of grief after his two older sons were killed on the same day, but his mother's kin play key roles in the romance. The Grail King is her brother and the Fisher King is her nephew, which means that the Fisher King is Perceval's cousin and the Grail King his uncle, although Chrétien does not spell out the relationships. The hermit is the brother of Perceval's mother, and thus also brother of the Grail King, which makes him the uncle of both Perceval and the Fisher King. Perceval's first cousin, who meets him in the forest just after he leaves the Grail castle, speaks of having dwelt in his mother's house and appears also to be a relative on his mother's side of the family. The Fisher King received the sword he gives Perceval from his blonde niece, who is perhaps in a relationship of second cousin to Perceval. The other important lineage in the romance is Arthur's, which includes his nephew Gawain.

Gawain's sister Clarissant and his unnamed mother live in the
Castle of the Rock of Champguin with his grandmother Ygerne,
who is also Arthur's mother and rules the castle.

The Castle of the Rock of Champguin appears to be a fortress
in the land of the dead, ruled by the white-haired Queen Ygerne
dressed in white brocade, who has been dead for sixty years
(see l. 8738), and her daughter, who has been dead for twenty,
and inhabited by, among others, a hundred gray-haired and a
hundred white-haired men. The name Champguin is composed
of two elements, one of Latin or British Celtic provenance,
champ "field," and the other of British Celtic origin, *guin* "white,
sacred." In Celtic lore white is the color of the dead and the
Otherworld is also known as the "land of the dead." That the
castle is subject to a taboo is shown by the queen's reluctance
to allow Gawain to leave it and the fact that Grinomalant is reluctant even to tell Gawain its name. Its most salient feature for
those who come upon it is that any man who enters must die,
a threat that Gawain is the first to overcome by passing the test
of the Magic Bed. Overtones of incest mark Gawain's visit to
Champguin, as his grandmother and his mother, unaware of his
identity, discuss the prospects of his marrying Clarissant, his
own sister.

In his other romances, Chrétien de Troyes shows a propen-
sity to construct episodes that in some way resonate with each
other. Gawain's adventure in Champguin illuminates obscure
characteristics of Perceval's Grail experience. The Grail castle
is inhabited by Perceval's kin just as Gawain's family live on
the Rock of Champguin, but while Champguin is ruled by two
queens, a mother and daughter, the Grail castle is ruled by a
father and son who are kings. Access to each is facilitated by
a man in a boat. In both castles the newcomer is subjected to a
test: Gawain would have died had he failed the test of the Magic

Bed, and Perceval is told by the hermit that he would have died except for his mother's prayer. Gawain observes running waters, broad plains, and forests filled with game in Champguin, but only after he has passed the test and attained sovereignty, at which point he is dressed in a white (ermine) robe. He is destined to recover the noble ladies' possessions and to free the castle from its enchantments, as Perceval would have done for his kin had he passed the question test.

There is also a suggestion of incest in Perceval's adventure in the Grail castle. His mother had told him that his father was wounded between the legs and as a consequence both his land and his treasure went into decline. Perceval's cousin explains that the Fisher King has been wounded between the haunches, and he lives in a land that is in a state of profound decline, a wasteland. Wounding between the legs is, as I have mentioned, a medieval circumlocution for castration: the king is sterile and his infirmity renders the land barren. Is it possible that the Fisher King, then, is Perceval's own dead father and the Grail King his grandfather? If this is so, then Perceval would be the offspring of incest between his mother and her nephew. Had Perceval been able to pass the test in the Grail castle, both the king and the land would have been healed. Was he then destined, like Gawain, to be installed as the new king of a familial enchanted castle after returning and asking the right questions? Although the last 2,700 lines of the romance, in the incomplete state in which we have it, concern exclusively Gawain's adventures, Chrétien no doubt planned to reintroduce Perceval into the narrative to fight a battle in which his cousin's prediction would be fulfilled, namely that the sword given him by the Fisher King would fail him. But the Hideous Damsel's prediction (ll. 4670–76) makes it unlikely that the Fisher King's health would have been restored.

In addition to these worldly concerns, *Perceval* has a spiritual aspect that sets it apart from Chrétien's other works. The prologue highlights Christian charity, the love of God and one's neighbor, to both of which the young Perceval must be initiated. Although his mother instructs him on what the church is, tells him to pray, and gives him a brief account of Christian beliefs, and although he does indeed pray for her health, Perceval eventually forgets God and does not enter a church for five years until the Good Friday on which he meets the penitents, one of whom again gives him a summary of the tenets of Christian faith. When last heard of in the romance, Perceval has learned again about Christ's death and has received the Eucharist from his uncle. One cannot help thinking that if he was to come again to the Grail castle and this time ask the questions, his correct conduct would have resulted from his spiritual progress.

Chrétien's unfinished *Perceval* exercised such a fascination that in eleven of the fifteen manuscripts it is followed, without a break, by continuations written between the final years of the twelfth century and around 1230. There are four continuations ranging in length from around 9,500 to more than 19,000 lines. The first two are anonymous (the second being falsely ascribed to Wauchier de Denain), the third is by a certain Manessier, and the fourth is by Gerbert de Montreuil.

The First Continuation, unfinished, carries forward the narration of Gawain's adventures and identifies the bleeding lance as the spear used to pierce the side of the crucified Christ. The Second Continuation takes up where the first ends, and breaks off with Perceval returning to the Grail castle. Manessier, who wrote for Jeanne, countess of Flanders, the grandniece of Chrétien's patron, has Perceval see the Grail procession a second time. He is crowned as the Fisher King's successor and upon his death the Grail, the lance, and the platter are transported to heaven. Gerbert's Fourth Continuation is an interpolation between the Second and Third Continuations. In both the First and the Third Continuations, the Grail is a vessel that produces food. In addition, prologues that have been given the titles *Bliocadran* and the *Elucidation* are included in some manuscripts. *Perceval* and its continuations and prologues make a compilation of more than 60,000 lines in most of the manuscripts, testimony to the power that Chrétien's tale exercised over its readers. The extent to which the continuators had access to independent versions of the Grail legend is a vexed question.

That Chrétien does not attach the epithet "holy" directly to the word *Grail* is important to note. He only has the hermit say, when mentioning the host that keeps the Grail King alive, that the Grail is "so holy a thing" (l. 6426). He does, however, confer on the Grail an aura of the sacred in the scene in which its approach fills the hall with a mysterious light and in which it is accompanied by candelabra in a procession. *Graal,* "grail," is a rare word in Old French, but we are fortunate to have a definition from the pen of an author who wrote about forty years after Chrétien, Helinand, who describes it as "a plate broad and somewhat deep."

The transformation of the Grail into the Holy Grail is the work of Robert de Boron, a Burgundian knight who is thought to have written his *Joseph of Arimathea* in verse around the year 1200. Robert identifies the Grail not as a serving dish but as the chalice of the Eucharist that Christ used at the Last Supper, given by Pontius Pilate to Joseph of Arimathea, who later used it to collect the blood of Christ as he took his body down from the cross. According to Robert's narrative, Joseph is imprisoned but stays alive miraculously without food or drink and Christ appears to him with the Grail in hand. When he is freed from captivity, Joseph travels with his sister Enygeus, his brother-in-law Bron, and a group of other Christians through many lands. In memory of the Last Supper, he establishes at the bidding of the Holy Spirit a ceremony in which the Grail, along with a fish, is placed on a table and those sitting at it who have led a chaste life and believe in the Trinity have all that they desire. Robert calls Bron the Rich Fisher because he is the one who catches the fish used in the Grail service. One seat at the Grail table is reserved for the future son of Bron; anyone else who sits in it will be swallowed up by the earth. Bron receives the Holy Grail from Joseph and travels west with it to the vale of Avalon, probably the region near Glastonbury in Britain. Robert de Boron does not mention the bleeding lance. Bron and Enygeus have a child, Alain, whose unnamed son will be the next keeper of the Grail.

According to another work, the prose Didot *Perceval,* which is thought to be the translation, with additions, of a lost poem by Robert de Boron, Bron's son Alain is Perceval's father. Bron is infirm but can be healed by Perceval. First, however, Perceval goes to King Arthur's court and sits at the Round Table in the Siege Perilous. The seat roars out and splits beneath him, and a voice declares that on account of his boldness in sitting in the seat, Bron will not be healed, the seat will not be rejoined, and the enchantments of Britain will not be lifted until a knight who surpasses all others in prowess asks what the Grail is and whom it serves. Perceval sets off in search of Bron's dwelling and reaches an analogue of Chrétien's Grail castle, where he sees

the Grail procession but fears to ask the questions because he
wants to be polite to the host. After meeting the weeping young
lady in the forest and confessing to his uncle the hermit, he encounters the Fisher King in his boat, revisits the Grail castle, and
does ask the questions, causing Bron to be cured. Bron instructs
Perceval in the secrets of the Grail before dying two days later.
The Siege Perilous is joined together and the enchantments
of Britain dissipate. There follows a brief account of Arthur's
conquest of Gaul, his battle with his nephew Mordred, and his
death. Whether Robert de Boron knew Chrétien's *Perceval* is
uncertain, although the author of the Didot *Perceval* surely did.

Yet another early example of French prose, *Perlesvaus, the
High Book of the Grail,* probably composed in the first decade
of the thirteenth century, builds on the Grail treatments of both
Chrétien and Robert de Boron and its anonymous author appears to have known Celtic traditions not reflected in those
authors. In *Perlesvaus,* the Fisher King is Perlesvaus's uncle,
who dies; the Grail castle has fallen into the hands of another
uncle, the pagan King of Castle Mortal, which has led to the
disappearance of the Grail and the implements that accompany
it. Perlesvaus reconquers the Grail castle, becoming thereby the
Grail King without having to ask any questions. After a great
battle in which he defeats the Black Hermit, Perlesvaus leaves to
assume rule over the Isle of Plenty. Also playing a role in the *Perlesvaus* is Lancelot's love for Guinevere, who dies in the course
of the romance. *Perlesvaus* is imbued with Christian typological
overtones and the crusading spirit, neither of which appear to
play a significant role in Chrétien's *Perceval.* Benedictine monas-
ticism is thought to have had a role in shaping the particular
forms of spirituality found in *Perlesvaus.*

On the basis of Chrétien's and Robert de Boron's works and
the Didot text, a vast compilation known as the Lancelot-Grail

Cycle was put together in the period 1220–30. This series of anonymous prose texts is also called the Vulgate Cycle because of its widespread popularity in the period, as evidenced by more than a hundred surviving manuscripts. It consists of the *Story of the Holy Grail* (a "prequel" written to bring the early tale of the Grail into line with the later parts of the compilation), *Merlin,* the *Lancelot* proper, the *Quest for the Holy Grail,* and the *Death of King Arthur.*

The *Quest,* suffused with monastic values, gives the most thoroughly Christian interpretation of the Grail myth of any medieval work. In the *Lancelot,* we learn that Lancelot has a son, Galahad, whose mother is the Grail maiden, daughter of the Rich Fisher King. Galahad is descended from both the biblical David and Joseph of Arimathea and belongs to the lineage of the Grail kings. At the beginning of the *Quest,* the newly knighted Galahad is led into Arthur's palace at Camaalot, where he passes the tests of the Siege Perilous and the Sword in the Stone, indications that as the best knight in the world he will fulfill the Grail quest. When the knights of the Round Table are seated in the hall, a clap of thunder sounds and they are all struck dumb as the Holy Grail, sent by God, floats into the room, and each guest is provided with whatever food he desires. Led by Gawain, each of the knights pledges not to rest until he is seated once again in a palace where such dishes are served daily. After a series of intertwined adventures in which most of the knights, including Lancelot and Lionel, fail in the quest because of their sinful lives, Galahad, Perceval, and Lancelot's cousin Bohort reach the Grail castle, Corbenic. There they participate with nine other knights in a Mass celebrated by Josephé, the son of Joseph of Arimathea, who has descended from heaven for the occasion, at a silver table on which the lance has been placed by angels alongside the Grail. The communion host used in the Mass takes on the appearance of a child and the crucified Christ emerges from the Grail to give the knights communion. Galahad heals the wounded King Pelles by anointing him with blood from the lance. Having seen the beatific vision, Galahad, now king of the land, dies, to be followed by Perceval a year later. The various components of the knights' quest for the Grail and the objects they encounter are assigned allegorical meanings in conformity with Christian ideas of grace and salvation, often articulated by monks dressed in the white habits of the Cistercian order whom the knights meet along the way and who expound ideas that can be linked to the writings of Saint Bernard of Clairvaux. The *Quest for the Holy Grail* is thought to have been written by a Cistercian or someone closely allied with that order.

Perceval's story became in the Middle Ages the basis of literary works in languages other than French: in the thirteenth century the Norse *Parcevalssaga* and *Valversthattr* and the *Perchevael* incorporated into a Flemish *Lancelot* in verse, and in the fourteenth century the English *Sir Perceval of Gales,* in which the Grail itself does not figure. Two adaptations, the Welsh *Peredur* and the Middle High German *Parzival,* are of special importance.

Peredur, Son of Efrawg, is one of three Welsh romances that appear to be influenced by Chrétien's work. Romances in this period were often experienced aurally, read out loud to aristocratic audiences, and *Peredur* may be based on the Welsh author's participation in such an event. Like the other Welsh romances, it incorporates Celtic motifs and incidents not found in French analogues. Among the differences from Chrétien's narrative are that the counterpart of the man who initiates Perceval into knighthood, Gornemant of Goort, is Peredur's maternal uncle. A second uncle has Peredur break a sword three times and put it back together twice. In the Grail procession, two young men bear the lance that bleeds profusely onto the floor. Most notably, the Grail itself, identified as a "salver" or serving dish borne by two young women, contains not a communion host but a man's head resting in a pool of blood, a sight that is accompanied by loud shrieking. After Peredur's visit to the equivalent of the castle of Beaurepaire and the scene of the blood drops on the snow, the Welsh romance departs radically from Chrétien's plot. Peredur falls in love with Angharad Golden-Hand and ceases speaking until she decides to give him her love. He then embarks on a series of adventures, including an encounter with a monster called the Addanc. Eventually he marries the empress of Constantinople and lives with her for fourteen years. Toward the end of the romance, he encounters a young man who declares that he had appeared to Peredur before in a number of guises, including that of one of the women in the Grail procession. The severed head, an element typical of Celtic tradition, belonged to an unnamed cousin of Peredur who was killed by the witches of Caer Loyw (Gloucester), who are also responsible for laming Peredur's uncle, the host of the Grail castle. With the help of Arthur's war-band, Peredur then kills the witches of Caer Loyw. This text dating from the end of the twelfth or the beginning of the thirteenth century was once thought to be a source of *Perceval* and may well contain elements that were a part of the original Celtic myth.

Wolfram von Eschenbach, a Bavarian knight who also wrote *Willehalm* and *Titurel,* drew upon Chrétien's *Perceval* and the First Continuation as well as other sources in writing his magnificent romance *Parzival* between 1200 and 1212. Although in

general Wolfram follows Chrétien's lead, he greatly embellishes
and expands the story to almost 25,000 lines. Wolfram charac-
terizes the Grail as a stone, carried by a chaste young woman:
when a communion wafer is placed on it, it is able to furnish
food in abundance for those in its presence. Two silver knives
are also carried in the Grail procession. A number of characters
who are anonymous in Chrétien are named by Wolfram, such
as the Fisher King (Anfortas), Parzival's mother (Herzeloide),
his father (Gahmuret), his cousin (Sigune, whom he encounters
four times rather than once as in Chrétien), and his hermit uncle
(Trevrizent). Parzival manages to return to the Grail castle,
Munsalvæsche, and succeeds Anfortas as Grail king. Wolfram
mentions Chrétien at the end of his romance, but gives greater
credit for the tale to another author, a problematic "Kyot the
Provençal" who may be fictive. *Parzival* was extremely popular
in the Middle Ages, as is testified by its survival in more than
seventy manuscripts.

From its origin in Chrétien's *Perceval,* the Grail myth was
taken up by an astonishing number of authors writing in a va-
riety of languages, a practice that was continued by such figures
as Alfred, Lord Tennyson and T. S. Eliot and persists up to the
present day. That each has given the mysterious object new
interpretations and a new symbolism only confirms Chrétien
de Troyes's power as one of the master storytellers of Western
tradition.

Recommended for Further Reading

Medieval Texts

Bryant, Nigel, trans. *The High Book of the Grail: A Translation of the Thirteenth-Century Romance of Perlesvaus.* Cambridge: D. S. Brewer; Totawa, N.J.: Rowman and Littlefield, 1978.

Hatto, A. T., trans. Wolfram von Eschenbach, *Parzival.* Harmondsworth: Penguin Books, 1980.

Jones, Gwyn, and Thomas Jones, trans. *The Mabinogion.* Everyman's Library. Rev. ed. New York: Dutton; London: Dent, 1974. [*Peredur*]

Matarasso, Pauline M., trans. *The Quest of the Holy Grail.* Harmondsworth: Penguin Books, 1969.

Raffel, Burton, trans. Chrétien de Troyes, *Cligès.* With an Afterword by Joseph J. Duggan. New Haven and London: Yale University Press, 1996.

———. Chrétien de Troyes, *Erec and Enide.* With an Afterword by Joseph J. Duggan. New Haven and London: Yale University Press, 1996.

———. Chrétien de Troyes, *Lancelot: The Knight of the Cart.* With an Afterword by Joseph J. Duggan. New Haven and London: Yale University Press, 1996.

———. Chrétien de Troyes, *Yvain: The Knight of the Lion.* With an Afterword by Joseph J. Duggan. New Haven and London: Yale University Press, 1987.

Rogers, John. *Joseph of Arimathea: A Romance of the Grail.* London: Rudolf Steiner Press, 1990.

Critical Studies

Busby, Keith. *Chrétien de Troyes: Perceval (Le conte du Graal).* Critical Guides to French Texts, 98. London: Grant and Cutler, 1993.

Cazelles, Brigitte. *The Unholy Grail: A Social Reading of Chrétien de Troyes's Conte du Graal.* Palo Alto, Calif.: Stanford University Press, 1996.

Frappier, Jean. *Chrétien de Troyes: The Man and His Work.* Translated by Raymond J. Cormier. Athens: Ohio University Press, 1982.

Kelly, Douglas. *Chrétien de Troyes: An Analytic Bibliography.* Research Bibliographies and Checklists, 17. London: Grant and Cutler, 1976.

———. *Medieval French Romance.* Twayne's World Authors Series, 838. New York: Twayne, 1993.

Lacy, Norris J. *The Craft of Chrétien de Troyes: An Essay on Narrative Art.* Davis Medieval Texts and Studies, 3. Leiden: Brill, 1980.

Loomis, Roger Sherman. *The Grail: From Celtic Myth to Christian Symbol.* New York: Columbia University Press, 1963; repr. Princeton: Princeton University Press, 1991.

Maddox, Donald. *The Arthurian Romances of Chrétien de Troyes: Once and Future Fictions.* Cambridge Studies in Medieval Literature, 12. Cambridge: Cambridge University Press, 1991.

Nagy, Joseph. *The Wisdom of the Outlaw: The Boyhood Deeds of Finn in Gaelic Narrative Tradition.* Berkeley: University of California Press, 1985.

Olschki, Leonardo. *The Grail Castle and Its Mysteries.* Trans. J. A. Scott and ed. Eugene Vinaver. Berkeley: University of California Press, 1966.

Topsfield, L. T. *Chrétien de Troyes: A Study of the Arthurian Romances.* Cambridge: Cambridge University Press, 1981.